# IN THIS COLLECTION

A group of students come under attack by a military force from the future in **INVASION**. To survive they must put their faith and trust in the unlikeliest of all people, a teacher who also happens to be a secret agent from another timeline.

In **GOLIATH IX**, something has gone wrong. A space convoy finds itself in jeopardy after dropping out of FTL in a nebula while on their way to a new homeworld.

Two teens seek out their friend while reflecting on how much things have changed as the world ends in **TABITHA**.

Off-worlders are warned: outer rim planets are not safe. Dreams are dashed on a doomed outer rim planet that is both beautiful and terrifying in **BATARAKALA**.

In **ROGUE MOON**, a new ship, a new captain, and an untested crew confront a galactic threat. A threat that may be intent on finishing what was first attempted twenty years earlier... the annihilation of the human race.

# OF SPACE & TIME

## A COLLECTION OF SCIENCE FICTION SHORT STORIES

### RAY LECARA JR

SYNER-G PUBLISHING

SEATTLE, WASHINGTON

The stories contained in *Of Space & Time: A Collection of Science Fiction Short Stories* are a work of fiction. Names, characters, businesses, places, events, locales, and incidents are either the products of the author's imagination or used in a fictitious manner. Any resemblance to actual events, locales, or persons—living or dead—is entirely coincidental.

Syner-G Publishing
Seattle, Washington
www.Syner-GPublishing.com

Printed in the United States of America

Book Jacket Design © SGP
Back Cover Image: c/o Deselect @ Pixabay
Interior: GraphicMama-team @ Pixabay; Piyapong
Saydaung @ Pixabay. All other images licensed
under Creative Commons Zero 1.0 Public Domain
License

*To Robert...*

*For a man who may be grounded, I've never
met a soul whose spirit soars as high as yours.
I honor you, my friend, and look forward to
witnessing your own grand adventure...
an adventure that I know is just
around the corner.*

*"What an astonishing thing a book is. It's a flat object made from a tree with flexible parts on which are imprinted lots of funny dark squiggles. But one glance at it and you're inside the mind of another person, maybe somebody dead for thousands of years. Across the millennia, an author is speaking clearly and silently inside your head, directly to you. Writing is perhaps the greatest of human inventions, binding together people who never knew each other, citizens of distant epochs. Books break the shackles of time. A book is proof that humans are capable of working magic."*

– Carl Sagan, *Cosmos*

Carl Sagan (1934-1996) was an American astronomer, planetary scientist, cosmologist, astrophysicist, astrobiologist, author, and science communicator

# TABLE OF CONTENTS

# INVASION

The power in the school flickered several times before finally going out, leaving the hallways cast in shadows of red emergency lighting.

There was no telling what caused the explosion, other than it was in the vicinity of the auditorium and main foyer. Screams of panic underscored the chaos.

Valerie made for the door. "Oh, my God! Mom! Mommy!"

Already a step ahead, Mr. Rustam, her seventh-grade teacher, caught the cheerleader by the waist. He thrust her thin, light frame back into the room. Traumatized by the surreal nature of the situation, the kids remained frozen in place.

Senses sharpening, Rustam's secret double-life training kicked in and he reflexively went about determining the source of the blast. Parts of the auditorium's wall to the right of the classroom — and part of what was the Tiger Team hallway — was destroyed. Black streaks, evidence of a detonation of some kind, now charred the previously grey concrete walls.

"Mr. Rustam, maybe we should..." Sam began before another explosion rocked the building. It shook the overhead lights and sent large cracks zigzagging through the walls.

This time the three students all responded alike. Nerves already frayed, they covered their heads and cowered low to the ground.

Rustam was now above them. "You guys trust me?"

"Wh-Why would you ask that?" Tai asked, almost too quietly to hear.

"Do you trust me?" Rustam asked again, this time meeting the eyes of each child. Slowly they nodded their heads. But he still wasn't sure how they would respond once out in the hall. "It's going to be very dangerous out there. You need to follow me and do exactly what I tell you. Okay?"

"What's... what's going on, Mr. Rustam?" Sam asked against the growing chorus of wailing from those caught in the blast. Beyond the destruction. It was the elephant in the room everyone was too shell shocked to address.

"We can figure that out later. Our immediate concern is getting out of here.

We need to get out of here now! But you all have to trust me and listen carefully if we're going to get out of here alive."

"I don't understand. What's happening?" Valerie asked, tears flowing in streaks over her cheeks smearing the makeup she wore for tonight's winter concert. "What about my parents?"

"I'm not sure what's happening," Rustam admitted, "and I know you're all worried about your families. Your classmates. But if I am going to keep you safe, we need to move."

Suddenly the rumbling returned, its vibrations shaking the entire building. Where it came from, Rustam couldn't be certain. Perhaps overhead. Judging by the intensity, whatever it was, it was drawing closer.

Rustam stepped out into the hallway as he roughly pulled black gloves over clammy hands. To the right, remnants of the Tiger Team corridor and entranceway to the main foyer gave him pause. How many times had he walked the hallway? How many times had he watched his students pass in the same hall on the way to class or to the bus?

Exposed wires sparked and popped in the darkness revealing twisted metal amid the piles of cinder block rubble and what used to be classrooms. For the sake of the students in his care, he was thankful the view of the foyer—and the chaos beyond—was blocked.

"Let's go. Stay close," Rustam said, leading the kids into the hallway. Then to the left.

The hall intersected with another a few feet down, with one other intersection some yards further beyond the next team. It was there that they could exit; that is, if they could make it out undetected.

Rustam inhaled sharply, grinding his teeth. This was no coincidence. His initial mission was to retrieve what was in the basement of the school only one floor down. It would seem the parameters of his mission had changed because the chances of being able to fetch his package while keeping the kids safe had been reduced from slim to none.

More than anything he wanted to call in reinforcements by activating his personal distress beacon. Perhaps that would give him the edge he needed. But without knowing who or what was outside, he feared exposing his position would put them all in even more danger. Whatever was happening, it was clear that it was an attack of some kind. Maybe even an invasion.

Pushing fearful thoughts aside, Rustam redirected his attention back to the kids. One dilemma at a time, he reminded himself. He hoped HAMIL-E was nearby in the event of an emergency extraction. Yet he couldn't prevent a wave of disgust from washing over him. While HAMIL-E served as Rustam's contact, he was also a well-respected advisor. Rustam swallowed hard, deeply ashamed by the fact that he had failed his mentor.

Keeping low, Rustam checked the hallway, readying the kids to run across when given the word.

A bright, white blinding light lit up the dark hallways, piercing the large glass windows of the building's front façade.

"That was quick," Tai exclaimed, watching the spotlight.

"Mr. R, I think they're looking for us," Sam said. There was hope in his voice. But that changed when he saw Rustam's distressed expression.

"Someone is looking for us all right, but it's not who you think."

This new wrinkle concerned Rustam. He had to get the kids out and away from the building.

"Go!" Rustam whispered. "Don't stop," he commanded as he waved his gloved hands, "until you get through the next team's hallway. We'll use those stairs to exit the building."

"But..." Valerie interrupted.

"But nothing. And don't you dare go any further. Not yet. And not without me. Just wait up. I'll be right behind you."

Valerie opened her mouth to say something else, but Rustam cut her off with, "Now go! Stay low!"

He knew it was a big ask to have them head in the opposite direction of their friends and family. It bothered him to see the fear in their young eyes, but there was no other way. They all needed to head away from the destruction.

Breathing a sigh of relief, he was grateful the collapsed debris blocked them from everyone else. The cries and screaming were enough.

The kids raced down the hall and disappeared under the cover of darkness. Muted emergency lights cast murky shadows that danced about as if they were alive.

With one final look to his rear, Rustam gingerly made his way across the hall. Having advanced no more than a couple of steps across, he was then violently tackled by a large assailant. The wind rushed from his lungs as his back was slammed against a stone wall.

The assailant laughed heartily. "Hello, little man!"

"Wallace?" Rustam managed with great difficulty.

It was only a couple of hours ago that he and Wallace had come face-to-face on the auditorium's rear catwalk overlooking the seated audience and stage. From there, they had the best view of the winter concert.

"Russ-tim, right," the substitute had asked then, extending a large, meaty hand.

But Rustam was intently watching the boy from his homeroom and Social Studies class, Sam Declan, play his guitar solo in the middle of a number the entire band was performing. He had also spotted Valerie McCall who was holding a flute. Off stage Rustam even noticed Tai Yeoh with a group of other young people dressed in the same black and white ensemble. Since Tai wasn't holding an instrument, he figured Tai probably sang.

"It's pronounced Roo-stum," the teacher corrected before removing his gloves to shake the sub's hand.

"Oh, sorry. Jake Wallace."

"Ahh, yeah. You're new, aren't you?"

Rustam had asked, pocketing his black gloves.

"Yep. Started subbing a few weeks ago. How about you? How long have you been a teacher here at Stoney Hill?"

Rustam remembered shrugging. "Hmm, going on six years, I think."

"Impressive," the sub had replied, leaning over the railing to closely inspect a group of young people below them.

Rustam recalled trying to size the sub up as best as he could: He was a young fellow, that much he could tell, maybe in his late 20s, early 30s. And big — Jake was football player big. His stature dwarfed Rustam's already diminutive frame that much more. Rustam couldn't help but wonder, as he turned to again watch the kids on stage, what kind of work the sub did before coming to Stoney Hill Middle School. Or if he had ever played college ball.

At present, Jake's large forearm was pressing against Rustam's windpipe, making it nearly impossible to speak. Or breathe. He held the teacher suspended nearly two feet from the floor.

"I'm curious, tiny man," the sub seethed. "Just how tall are you? Three feet? Four?"

Reaching the end of the hall, the kids were horrified to discover their teacher wasn't with them.

"I thought he said he'd be right behind us," Valerie complained as she caught her breath.

Squinting, Tai tried to make out the two figures obscured in the blackness outside their classroom. "Hey, isn't that one of the substitute teachers with Mr. Rustam?"

It was difficult to make anything out in the shadows, even with the intermittent flashes of white lights from outside.

Valerie suddenly screamed, startling the boys in response.

Wallace was leaning into Rustam as Valerie's screams reverberated off the walls of the hallway. He was so close to Rustam, Rustam couldn't escape Wallace's feculent breath. "Lemme get to the point," he said, his black beady pupils deeply set in sockets of sweaty nearly purple flesh. "You have something I want. The device. I want it. And I want it NOW!"

"Mr. Rustam!" one of the kids yelled.

Rustam cursed silently to himself. He knew better. Why hadn't he and HAMIL-E anticipated the presence of students in any of their planned scenarios? Why hadn't they planned on the possibility that the intel was faulty? Putting any one of the kids in danger should never have been an option.

Hot spittle sprayed from Wallace's lips as he uttered his threat. "Don't make me ask you again!"

Rustam could hardly breathe; floating spots of darkness seemed to multiply as Wallace's forearm pressed harder against his larynx, further restricting air from his lungs.

As the world slipped away, Rustam focused all his energy on slowly drawing his legs up to his chest. In a desperate attempt to disarm his opponent, Rustam thrust his legs outward into Wallace's sternum.

Jake Wallace exhaled loudly. Then grinned. The kick had been unexpected. Before Wallace could fully recover — which Rustam knew was only seconds away — Rustam thrust another, more direct kick, into Wallace's mid-section. The substitute doubled over.

Once free from the forearm, Rustam ducked low and rolled to the left. Up on one knee, he reflexively pulled back the sleeve of his coat to draw his weapon: an armband beamer.

But he was a beat too slow.

By the time Rustam was up and armed, he could see, illuminated by the bright, search light from outside the windows, Wallace already had his own weapon drawn.

It was now a draw — a test — to see who would fire first.

Accompanying the light, a loud growing hum caused the remaining three-story collection of ornate glass pane — visible where the open second floor hall section crossed over the intersecting first floor hallway — to rattle. From either floor, the front façade of the building's midsection was visible. With all the glass, the view of the ball fields just outside and woods beyond was a sight to behold during the day. Under the cover of night this February evening, the only thing visible outside where lights of various colors and shapes moving in the sky and on the ground.

There was no mistaking the thrumming noise. The hum quickly grew into a whine and was then followed by a spattering of laser fire.

At the end of the hallway, Valerie was screaming for Rustam. Sam, however, stood still. In shock. Feeling powerless, he didn't know what to do. Was there anything he *could* do?

It was Tai who acted. Without warning, he took off back towards the classroom.

Emerging from the shadows Rustam noticed Tai's tiny frame moving in fast. Abandoning his stance before Wallace,

Rustam was up and running to meet the boy, catching him mid-stride just as laser fire scorched the entire area followed by an unmistakable thunk, thunk, thunk.

"Clocks!" the teacher explained over the noise. "Hold on!"

Luckily Tai was a light, small boy for a seventh grader. With the boy slung over his shoulder, the teacher quickly advanced down the hallway towards the others.

"Get down! Get. Down," he yelled.

Rustam's fingers fumbled over his utility belt. He knew he had only seconds to activate his PIN — a personal impermeable net just big enough to cover the four of them. It activated as the hall lit up in a blinding flash of bright colors accompanied by a loud explosion. The detonation's wave of intense heat knocked them all hard to the floor.

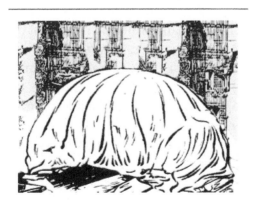

# [ 2 ]

Rustam coughed. It was the only sound he was aware of in the darkness. They were safe under the protective blanket the teacher had activated. Bits of tile, wires, and concrete rolled freely from the netted material as Rustam slowly rose, pulling the covering from himself and the kids.

All was still, silent, but the ringing in his ears. Rustam looked down at his watch. How long had they been out? Judging by the thin plumes of smoke rising from the surrounding rubble, it hadn't been long.

On one knee, he patted Tai on the shoulder. He was sure the kids would be even more disoriented than he was.

"Tai? Tai, buddy. You okay?"

Tai jerked awake and immediately began crying. Rustam adjusted Tai's spectacles, which were half off his face. But Tai didn't seem to know or care what Rustam was doing; he leapt for Rustam, embracing him tightly. Burying his face into Rustam's coat, he sobbed tears of fear and exhaustion as the others came to.

Sam blinked hard, fighting back the liquid that was pooling in his own eyes. With a sooted hand, Sam executed a quick wipe before Valerie took notice. Rustam acknowledged Sam and nodded as if to silently ask, "Are you okay?"

Motioning an affirmative, Sam set about assisting Valerie.

"Don't touch me," she hissed. "Keep your hands off of me!"

Sam recoiled as if bitten by a venomous snake. "I—I was only trying to help."

Ignoring Sam, she held up her right arm with disgust. "Aw, wonderful! Just great! This blouse is torn! Ugh, and my charm bracelet is missing! I don't believe this." Noticing Tai crying, she added, "I don't need your help, Bottoms. I'm not a baby like Mouse over here."

"Leave him alone, Val," Sam said as he stood, brushing the dust from his pants.

Tai wiped his eyes with blackened fingers and adjusted his glasses before standing.

Valerie nearly tripped trying to stand on her own. This only infuriated her even more. "No, I won't." She motioned to Tai, "Like he's the only one in this mess?"

"That's not fair and you know it," Sam countered quietly. He ran his hands through his hair before pushing back some of the long strands from his eyes. This was no time for theatrics, of which Valerie was all too well known for.

"Are you two all right?" Rustam asked, attempting to break the tension.

Valerie wasn't. "What is going on? Just what is going on?" she demanded.

"Yeah, what was that?" Sam asked, helping Tai navigate some of the debris.

Wiping the settling dust from his bald head, the teacher replied matter-of-factly, "Clocks." And then upon noticing the puzzled expressions of his students, he corrected himself. "Bombs."

Sam was stupefied. "Bombs?"

"Who would try to bomb the school?" Tai asked.

Valerie scoffed. "Oh, please! Terrorists? In Stoney Hill? Yeah, right!" When Rustam failed to contradict her assumption, she added, "What? You mean this really was a terrorist attack?"

Rustam pursed his lips. "In some ways that's not entirely incorrect."

Valerie wiped her eyes before rolling them, smearing her mascara even more. She was tired. Agitated.

"Well, I always thought you were a freak for a teacher. I see it's been confirmed." After a slightly exaggerated cough, she demanded, "Now, where's my mom and dad?"

The teacher could offer very little at the moment. As the ringing in his ears subsided, it gave way to new sounds: the faint sounds of movements around — maybe even in — the building.

And the sound of engines. Aircraft.

He turned to the girl. "I'm afraid it's not going to be that easy, Va—"

"I think they're directly above us," interrupted an electronic voice coming from the floor beneath them. "Check any and all heat signatures for the one identified as the agent."

Sam snapped his head in Rustam's direction.

"Agent," Sam repeated, scrunching up his facial features in disbelief.

"They're probably referring to the other guy, dork!" Valerie dismissed. "Like, Mr. Rustam could actually be an agent."

"Actually, there's a lot you don't know about me," Rustam responded against the sound of Valerie's phony laugh. Then again, there was a lot *he* didn't know about himself, either. Amnesia will do that to you.

The kids watched as Rustam surveyed the area, first with surprise and then suspicion. The building was in ruins. It was becoming increasingly more dangerous to remain inside. They were lucky to be alive.

"Is... is there something you should be telling us?" Sam asked, shivering. He didn't think it was possible to feel any more frightened or bewildered.

"Wha—what is that thing on your arm?" Tai asked, distracting Rustam for the moment.

The teacher smiled, grateful for the change in subject.

"It's actually on my wrist." He took a moment to pull back his coat sleeve. "It's a weapon that can emit a laser beam. It's called a beamer."

Though Valerie and Sam skittered back, Tai's eyes lit up for the first time all evening. He laughed out loud, forgetting for the moment where he was and what had just happened. "That's soooooo cool!"

"Yeah, it is," Rustam conceded with a half-grin. "I'll happily tell you more about it later. First, we have to get out of this building."

"Because we're under attack?" Sam asked.

"It's an alien invasion," Tai realized. Jerking his head to read Rustam's face, he added, "Right? That's what it is. Aliens."

The teacher turned to Sam, disregarding the comments about attacks and aliens. "Sam, I need you to hold on to Valerie and quietly lead everyone upstairs. I'm afraid exiting downstairs right now isn't an option."

"I don't need to be held on to," Valerie defensively charged. Then she let fly with, "In fact, I wouldn't be surprised if," and she pointed at Rustam, "*you* were the terrorist."

The kids all paused in place. Valerie had a point.

"Help! We're up here," she shouted loud enough for the intruders below to hear.

"Val!" Tai shrieked. "Why did you—? They'll hear us!"

"What is your problem, you little monkey? It's obvious the Marines have come to rescue us."

"I don't want to get eaten," Tai gasped. "Mr. R!"

Valerie rolled her eyes and exhaled loudly. "It's *not* aliens," she countered emphatically. "Aliens aren't going to talk like us. It's the Marines."

The teacher was exasperated but held silent. Time was running out. Too many things had already gone wrong. Between the building's reduced structural integrity and whatever was advancing towards them, the longer it took for them to evacuate the building, the more limited their options were going to be.

"That quickly, huh? Marines? Really?" Sam asked Valerie. He then searched his teacher's eyes. "Are you really some kind of terrorist?"

Time stood still as all eyes fell accusingly on Rustam.

No, he wasn't a terrorist. But what could he say? He was partly responsible for whatever was happening. Was he supposed to admit to being a secret agent? A green one at that! From a future timeline.

Sam held his teacher's gaze. He recognized sorrow. Sadness. He had seen it before. In his mother's eyes. Something like that was impossible to hide.

From under the debris, Tai pulled something out, shook it and then handed it to Rustam. It was Rustam's fedora. "He's not a terrorist, you guys. He's our Social Studies teacher."

Rustam gave Tai's shoulder a gentle squeeze, smiling gratefully. Putting the hat on, he then said, "Look, those guys coming upstairs are not Marines. Far from it..."

"See," Tai said looking to Valerie. "I told you. Aliens."

"No, not aliens, either," Rustam assured.

"Duh," Valerie quipped smacking her palm against Tai's forehead. Turning to her teacher while Tai rubbed his brow, she was determined to get some answers. "Then, like, who are they?" she demanded, hands on her hips.

"There'll be time for explaining later... or at least I hope there will be. Right now you three need to get upstairs as fast as you can. I'll be following closely behind."

Valerie scoffed. "Right. Just like before?"

Rustam nodded. "Point taken. I just need to make sure of something."

Sam looked worried.

Rustam put his hands on Sam's shoulders. "Don't worry, Sam. I'm no terrorist. But what's happened here today is big! Very, very big. It'll be okay, though. I promise. Just, please... please get up there as fast as you can."

Sam signaled to Tai. "C'mon, Mou—," he started to say before correcting himself, "I mean, Tai. C'mon, Tai." How he hated middle school nicknames. A victim of name-calling himself, he cursed inwardly for using a nickname he was sure Tai didn't like on account of it calling attention to his size and his features. He hoped Tai hadn't heard him.

Grabbing a hold of Valerie's wrist, Sam tried to lead her up the stairs. She yanked her hand free, reluctant to follow. He wondered at that moment why Valerie never had a nickname. A few were coming to mind.

As the attack proved, Rustam's mission was compromised. He wasn't the only one who wanted the device that was purportedly buried somewhere under the building. And whoever it was that wanted the device, he was sure they weren't from this timeline. Not with the technology they possessed.

Rustam watched the kids ascend the stairs. The realization of what this enemy force was willing to go through to get it violently gripped him. As the surge of emotions transitioned from fear to anger to steely resolve, his gloved hands balled into clenched fists. Straightening up, he pulled back his shoulders in an alerted stance determined to protect his students at all costs. Even if it meant sacrificing his own life.

# GOLIATH IX

**P**assengers watching the shuttle craft about to moor itself alongside the civilian ship GALAXY III held their breath. Everyone was still on edge, as docking procedures took much longer than was accustomed to these days. A consequence of navigating an uncharted nebula after coming out of a faster-than-light jump.

Waiting for arrivals to disembark the shuttle craft, a young woman nervously worked to control the uncooperative strands of frizzy hair atop her head. Reflected in the side console within the hallway wall, her exaggerated features only heightened her anxiety ahead of her new assignment.

Even in the coolness of the docking station, with recycled air blowing about, sweat saturated the under part of her arms. Following the others in line before her, she climbed aboard the shuttle feeling the beads of perspiration run down her neck under her hair line.

"Ramos." Her name came out hoarsely, sounding foreign and much older than she actually was. Clearing her throat, she repeated her name as she held up her D.I.D. — a Digital Interface Device. "Rachel Ramos. I've been requested aboard the YUÀN BÓ."

An attractive boy not much younger than Rachel, wearing a Shuttle Authority badge and GOLIATH embroidered patch, scanned her digital device before giving her a look over.

"Remove your glasses," he instructed, preparing to scan her retina.

The shuttle clerk before Rachel guessed the tiny girl to be barely a hundred pounds. He smugly smiled at her as he performed his scan. If he really wanted to know her exact weight — or anything about her — he could easily call up her records. A perk he stumbled upon when he took the job, a job the machines usually performed before they became inoperable.

"So, you're a YUÀN BÓ teacher?"

"I am," the grinning young woman replied, immediately embarrassed by her all-too-obvious exuberance.

"Hope you know what you're in for," the boy said as he arched his eyebrows. Rachel thought she saw the corners of his mouth curl, as if he found the situation amusing knowing something she didn't. "You can have a seat over there," he said, directing her to an adjacent waiting room. "We'll be departing shortly."

Rachel brushed off the experience with a courtesy smile. Still mistaken for a teen, Rachel stood not much more than five feet. Having grown up around people who doubted her capabilities, she was used to it. This teaching assignment was a chance to prove them all wrong.

"Hey," the boy called out as Rachel made her way to the sitting area. "Ramos, is it?"

Rachel nodded. It was then she noticed his dimples.

"You're not related to Captain Ramos, are you?"

"I am," she answered with a smirk, jutting her chin forward with pride. "He's my father."

The boy's reaction was not what she expected. Clearly unimpressed, he acknowledged her with a snort. "Guess that explains how you got your assignment," was his response. Leaving Rachel stunned and speechless, he then pivoted to the entranceway to receive the remaining boarding parties.

Rachel stood frozen in place feeling as if she had just been slapped across the face. A heat worked its way up her neck and into her cheeks. It was the heat of embarrassment. Feeling the eyes of the other passengers on her, she made her way to the sitting area with her head down and took a window seat. Her nostrils flared as the heat of shame turned to anger, reddening her cheeks.

Humiliated, it took every ounce of willpower to keep from getting up to either confront the shuttle clerk or report him. The first time on a shuttle by herself, this wasn't something she was expecting. A third option made her smile in triumph. She would tell her father.

From her window seat, she could observe some of the ships that made up the colony's convoy. Her destination was a space vessel slightly behind this group of ships surrounding the GALAXY III. Illuminated only by the lights of transport ships, there were no close stars where they were. No other sources of light. Unlike where the YUÀN BÓ still remained, the space here appeared as a black canvas. It was an empty, endless void.

Sighing, she closed her eyes and leaned her head back as the dockmaster announced an update to the shuttle's departure. It wouldn't be long before she'd be able to settle into her own shuttle stateroom for the duration of her trip.

\* \* \*

Arriving at the YUÀN BÓ some twelve hours later, Rachel was surprised at how rested she felt. Those with long travel times were able to enjoy a bit more hospitality thanks to the tiny staterooms. If they could afford it. With several drop off and pick up points before her destination, the stateroom offered her a chance to nap, have some privacy, and even enjoy a bit of nourishment.

Entering the East Wing Magistrate's Office via the East Wing Docking Bay, Rachel was greeted by a heavyset receptionist with a blue beehive hairdo and horned rimmed glasses. Perhaps not so much greeted as spoken to.

"Just give it a moment. It lags at times," the receptionist said without a smile or glance in Rachel's direction. In fact, none of the four people in the office even registered her presence aside from the hologram atop a cold gray counter.

For the next ten minutes the interactive three-dimensional bust ran Rachel through digital forms, schedule details, and class expectations.

"... whi-whi-which you will fuh-fuh-find at compartment one seventeen," the hologram finished.

"Oh, okay," Rachel replied. "Uh... where do I go again?"

"Compart-ment-ment-ment one, one, seven," said the hologram.

Rachel licked her dry lips, darting her attention from the holo rep to the blue-haired human who seemed to be going out of her way to neglect her. "Um, yes. But how do I get there exactly?"

"Compartment one, one, seven. Lower leh-leh-level," came the holo's reply, its form blinking on and off with each word.

"Just follow the Yellow Line. Take the tubes to Deck 105," the blue-haired woman chimed in without looking up. "You'll be covering for Mr. Jebrah."

"And my things," the girl asked.

"They will be delivered to your temporary residence where they will be waiting for you after today's classes."

It was still rather new to engage by way of in-person human interaction. Before the incident in the nebula, most everything on their voyage was done using artificially enhanced androids. While much of the tech in the fleet still appeared salvageable, the recent growing reliance on manual human efforts could no longer be denied.

This was after decades of regulated human contact. The passage of the Universal Virus Anti-Proliferation Act in response to the Chandra Contagion was one of the last major decisions made by the now defunct United Nations before the journey into space to a new home became a necessity.

Everyday there were more reminders of how grim things had become for a fleet of mortal beings on a journey into the unknown that had begun before Rachel was born and would not be completed for at least another two generations. What she and people her age did today was for tomorrow and those yet to be born.

A vocal group of students could be heard from behind Beehive's screen. Their loud and boisterous banter soon erupted into laughter and applause.

Rachel smiled inwardly, the sound of merriment melting away her anxiety. "Thank you," she said turning to leave. "I think I am all set."

Just as the door to the hallway slid open, the speakers crackled with the sound of a male yelling at the top of his lungs. Though Rachel couldn't make out the words, the unmistakable tone was one of anger before it turned desperate. What followed were a series of shrieks. From the adult.

Ready to witness the office aflutter with activity to address the peril they had all just heard, Rachel was horrified by their passivity. No one moved. No one *was* moving. No one but the lady with blue hair. But her sloth-like response to the situation signaled a disconcerting cool detachment. None of what transpired on the screen seemed to shock the staff, much less her.

Deeply troubled by the scene, Rachel was about to protest when Ms. Beehive touched a button at the same time she spoke. "Requesting assistance. Come in Oh Ah," she said, presumably shortening the O and A in Office Authority, as in the Office Authority of YUÀN BÓ. This, Rachel learned from her earlier holo rep rundown, was their internal security and defense force.

Sensing Rachel's stare, the older woman turned her large head to the younger. "What're you still doing here?" she barked. "Well, teacher? Don't you have somewhere to be?"

Embarrassed, Rachel hastily pivoted and made for the hall, nearly slamming face first into the automated sliding doors. Following the Yellow Line, she shuffled quickly down the hallway.

A loud bell — no, buzzer — sounded. The klaxon echoed in her head until she reached the transport tubes. It seemed to be in sync with the thumping sensation in her chest.

Perspiration trickled along her spine as she regained her composure in the conveyor carriage. This was not how she imagined her first day.

Reaching Deck 105, Rachel exited into an overcrowded maze of listless youth of varying ages. Students blocked her path at every turn and failed to respond to any attempt to engage. For every right or left she took, she felt several more boxing her in.

Glancing Compartment 104 on her right, she was confident she wasn't far from where she needed to be. But space was limited in the narrow hallway, making her feel extremely constricted and claustrophobic. Although everyone *seemed* to be moving, they walked slow enough to appear standing still.

In a moment of clarity, Rachel wondered if the oxygen generator for this area of the ship was working to capacity. She made a mental note to report it to her father. It was certainly plausible the young people were being affected by low oxygen levels.

Unable to see past the wall of students blocking her, Rachel decided to tailgate a group of teens effortlessly gliding by.

Eyeing Compartment 126, she engaged her D.I.D. with a shaky hand, confirming the station she was to report to.

"Can I help you," an aged bony woman asked. Her sudden appearance startled Rachel. White as an apparition, she was a stark contrast to Rachel's own darker complexion.

Perhaps even more alarming was the woman's clothing. She wore a threadbare cotton dress of muted greens and blues. The dress, much too long for her, hung loosely from her frail boney frame.

"C'mon, dear. We haven't got all day. Classes are about to begin." The elder smiled, her pale thin skin taut against visibly jutting cheekbones. But it was a forced smile. Artificial.

"Of course," Rachel replied, feeling uncomfortable. Exposed. Vulnerable. She wanted to be in her classroom. "I'm just not sure where to... I'm just not sure *how* to get to where I am supposed to be."

"Who is the teacher you are replacing, dearie?"

"Jebuh something," was all Rachel could recall, frazzled.

"Mr. Jebrah, dear. Mr. Jebrah used to operate out of Compartment 117."

Rachel was confused. "Right. Um... Where is that again? I thought it was right off the tube, but I've been following the Yellow Line and I'm just not sure I am..."

"Dear, Compartment 117 is in the basement."

"Basement? The ship has a basement?"

"It's not an actual basement, dearie. It's just the term we use here for the lower level."

"How do I get to the basement then?"

"Follow the Yellow Line to the end. There's a ramp at the end of the initial hallway that drops to the lower level."

Rachel's expression said it all, striking the woman in front of her as comical.  She erupted with a dry laugh.

"It's a design flaw.  It doesn't help that several stations are not numbered consecutively.  Some of these ships, in fact, were not built for what the fleet has needed to outfit them for.  Now go on.  You have just enough time to make it."

* * *

Finding her station, Rachel witnessed students wildly out of control.  Even before she reached the room, the commotion could be heard down the hall.  She prayed with every step closer that the din wasn't coming from *her* group of students.

When she entered, Rachel found students playing virtual holo games with the safeties off.  That much was certain because of the damage done to the room and the bloodied condition she found some of the participants.

Afraid to turn her back to the raucous bunch, the young woman kept her back to the wall as she made her way to the room's Holo Smart Screen.  Teachers, per standard protocol, were instructed to sync their D.I.D.s with the screen. But Rachel hadn't yet been given clearance. Since the tech itself was working on limited capacity, it didn't matter much. It was one of the many things relied on in the past but no longer operational.

Inhaling unsteadily, Rachel closed her eyes to determine her next move.

To her dismay, when she opened her eyes the children, younger than she believed them to be just moments ago when she walked in, were now seated at stations throughout the room. With their D.I.D.s off, they met her perplexed reaction with inquisitive, bright glances. A yearning emanated from their expressions, tugging on Rachel's maternal desire to teach. To share her love of math. And of space. To reach those who felt lost or ignored.

Rachel drew her name on the surface of Mr. Jebrah's interactive table desk. It instantly displayed on the HSS behind her. It was then that Rachel noticed a child in the rear right corner of the room. He was near the slit in the far wall that served as a window to the unearthly hues set against the dark beyond. Rachel couldn't help but wonder what he saw, what his perception was of the many ships clustered in the remnants of the nebula. She wondered what he was thinking. Dreaming.

She smiled broadly. In that moment, she sought to communicate to the boy that he could be anything — have anything — he wanted so long as he put his mind to it. Behind her beaming white toothy smile, Rachel believed she was conveying that he would get all he wished for. That his time aboard these ships, as part of the fleet, would foster a greater community. Through a remembrance of what came before, ingenuity *and* sacrifice would never be forgotten. It would be preserved for his kids and his grandkids, and then on through their bloodlines and generations to come.

*Humankind*, she thought to herself with unbridled confidence, *would survive because of people like this boy and his peers.*

It was at that point he caught her gaze.

*No, not just survive. Flourish.*

Nodding, the child seemed to validate her thoughts. His signal conveyed that, *yes*, he understood everything to be okay.

But unlike many of the students seated before her, Rachel was raised in a protected cocoon of privilege shielded from the horrific realities of space colony life.

Coming to stand in front the table desk, the young teacher hoisted herself to sit atop the flat surface before a class seemingly rapt with attention. Removing her glasses,

Rachel rubbed at her eyeballs, sensing a dull ache in the back of her head — a remnant that had been with her since coming out of cryo when she was a young girl. Happily, against the silence of the room, she began volunteering background details about herself. She followed with what it was like growing up on GALAXY III, one of ten glorious Galaxy Class starships in the fleet. Turning to the thin slatted windows she looked far beyond the other ships suspended in space alongside the YUÀN BÓ, as if trying to find something in the space of colored gasses as she expressed her hopes and dreams for the colony.

She surprised herself with her concluding thoughts — a message of a rosy future not too far removed from the indoctrination they had all grown up with.

It was a message that was repeated on all the ships in the fleet. Only now, older and about to embark on this new position of educator, did she seem to get it, even if a growing number of those within the member states didn't. Factions within the colony had come to view the messaging as propaganda, especially following the events in the nebula.

Rachel closed her eyes and exhaled. Her anxiety was gone. She felt one with the universe. With those in the room. She was at peace.

Long were her thoughts held silent. As the daughter of a Galaxy Class starship captain, she was held to a very high standard. Because of this, she always had to act a certain way, talk a certain way. Rachel viewed her youth as a lost childhood. Neither seen nor heard, she didn't have a voice if it didn't echo her father's.

"I know what it's like to be a disappointment in the eyes of your parents," Rachel shared. "My father wanted a son, not a daughter."

Sharing her thoughts and feelings now, at this moment, felt natural. Safe. It was okay to be vulnerable before these kids — a feeling she hadn't expected.

A jolt violently rocked the ship. It was followed by an even stronger one.

Opening her eyes, Rachel's sense of peace turned to terror as heads and bodies began colliding. Blending. Morphing. They merged into hideous deformed monstrosities. Grins stretched off melting faces. Unblinking eyes, their centers pools of black, vacantly stared back at her. Some popped out from their sockets and rolled about on the floor.

Fear quickly returned, knotting her stomach and icily squeezing the air from her lungs. She raced behind the table for cover. Was the horror she was witnessing a space anomaly? Something with the ship's life support? An effect of the nebula? A malfunction of the FTL drive? Hunched over her D.I.D., she searched frantically for the proper response that followed protocol.

"It's going to be okay. We're going to figure this out."

A growing shadow loomed over her as she tried to contact the office.

"What's the matter, Rachel," an approaching student asked.

"It's Ms. Ramos," Rachel corrected without looking because she was so focused on accessing the proper information.

"Naw. I prefer Rachel," a large muscular girl said as she came into full view. She was so broad that she cast a dark shadow as she stood over Rachel. Squatting, she then added, "Besides, Ms. Ramos makes you sound old. Stuffy. You are way too fine for that, Ray-Ray."

Rachel momentarily pinched her eyes shut as the stress of the moment triggered a painful jabbing sensation from behind her eyeballs. She was so close to the student she could feel the girl's hot breath.

Appearing much older than the others, this girl looked to be nearly twenty years old. Rachel noted that she was dressed in GOLIATH garb. GOLIATH IX specifically.

"Th-The others?" Rachel asked. "My students?"

"They're fine." The student smiled. "You act like you've seen a ghost."

"But how..." Rachel gasped. "They were just... and GOLIATH." She pointed at emblem worn by the girl. "GOLIATH IX never made it through."

"Are you sure about that?"

"It's not possible..."

"And why is that?" the other asked. "Is it because you left us all to die?"

Rachel jerked her head from side to side. "I don't understand what you're talking about. We tried to save you."

"Really? Then explain why only certain ships in the fleet are forced to ration air, food, supplies? Why is there a class of elitist families with accommodations aboard their fancy yachts allowing them to continue living as if nothing ever happened to bring us out here in the first place?"

"That's not true," Rachel replied to the haunting visage.

"Isn't it? Tell me, Ray-Ray, where did you go to school?"

Her question put Rachel on the defensive. The teacher opened her mouth to answer but there were no words. The girl from GOLIATH IX had a point. Because her family could afford the extra credits, Rachel was privately schooled and never had to come aboard the YUÀN BÓ. Nor did her parents or grandfather. Come to think of it, even most of the tech was still operational on Rachel's ship.

And rationing? GALAXY III's idea of rationing came in the form of two meals a day versus the usual three. There was never any want... for food, air, or any other comforts for that matter.

*Because you have them already*, the words screamed in her head. *You've always had them.*

The student stood and crossed her bulging arms, a look of satisfaction across her face. "That's what I thought. So much for equal representation. Equal sacrifice."

Rachel stood too, determined to counter the student's claims when her D.I.D. slipped from her hand. The sound of it shattering as it hit the floor drew her attention. Reaching to pick up the pieces, Rachel was violently pushed from behind. Falling into the underside of the digital table desk, she lost her glasses hitting her head on a conduit box.

"That's not good," she whispered when she attempted to stand. Unaware of the blood seeping from a head wound, she felt woozy. She registered the sound of tittering and snickering as multiple shapes closed in around her. Without her glasses to see, their faces were nothing more than blurry demons.

Bells rang, distracting everyone before all hell broke loose.

She heard a fight start up in the back of the room. Amid the sounds of screaming, Rachel dropped to the floor once more to find her glasses. Waving away her young assailants with one hand, she fumbled for the frames with the other.

Though one eye was swollen, full of blood and tears that ran down her face, she retrieved her glasses in time to witness Authority-issued Space Steel blades entering flesh and slashing faces. Shades of crimson splattered the room's bone-colored partitions.

Rachel gasped at the melee, fearing the worst. "Where did you get those?" she yelled across the room. "Stand down. You're going to kill someone."

Klaxons blared in the distance. A buzzing noise, too.

Something hit one of the windows.

*Disrupter fire?*

An intricate web splintered the now compromised paned glass.

Rachel inhaled sharply, fear taking hold and constricting her chest. She gulped for air in short spurts. Her ribs ached from the violent heaving. Hyperventilating, she felt as if her heart had few moments to go before exploding within her rib cage.

*If something were to happen,* she thought to herself.

*If the window shattered...*

*If the ship was damaged...*

*If people died...*

She'd never come back from something like that. Her father would be shamed. Probably lose his command of GALAXY III. Because the students aren't just from one GOLIATH ship but from several ships throughout the fleet, this would be a transnational incident.

*But those from GOLIATH IX are dead.*

Against a cacophony of taunting laughter, she remembered the woman in the office and the kids on screen out of control.

"The Office Authority," she said aloud. "Stop or I am going to call Office Authority."

But there was no way to contact them since her D.I.D. was in pieces on the floor.

"Now, what seems to be the problem, Miss Ramos? Perhaps I can help."

Dressed in a tattered military uniform accentuated with large scuffed black military issued boots, Rachel found herself face-to-face with the once young student who had given her the "okay" sign with a nod earlier. Only now the boy appeared to be a young man. With dimples. The cute young man looked familiar. Bearing the same patch of her previous assailant, the emblem was a GOLIATH logo with a number corresponding to his ship — also the GOLIATH IX. Among the many different ships in the colony, most civilians lived aboard one of the thirty GOLIATH class vessels.

*Used to*, Rachel reminded herself with a shudder.

As the lad drew near, his face transformed into a dark angry shadow of its former self. At close proximity, his long black hair barely covered a series of ear piercings in his right ear. His hair was slick with grease. Matted. Congealed. His eyes red. Moist.

Clutching the teacher's hair in one hand, he drew her forward and down to her knees.

"It appears, Rachel Ramos, your position has been terminated. You are just too far out of your element."

Rachel protested. Not with her voice, but with a stream of tears.

"What we've learned from our experience in the nebula," the boy explained, "is that the future does *not* belong to us all."

"No," Rachel sobbed.

"How pathetic we were to believe in the lie 'sacrifice for *all*.' Disregard the comforts taken for granted on Earth Prime for the sake of 'future generations' we were told over and over."

"Y-yes. All of us," the teacher stammered.

"Really, Rachel? You pampered brat. What do you know about sacrifice? Have you watched a loved one waste away from cosmic radiation sickness? Seen the effects of overexposure to the vacuum of space? Have any of your family or friends suffered from oxygen deprivation? Space dementia?" Grinding his teeth, the young man shook his head. "So many people lost. Abandoned. Cast aside. And it is *we* who keep the fleet moving."

"I'm so sorry," Rachel whispered.

"Would you so willingly give up your coddled life for, let's say, a group of people you've never met on GOLIATH IX?"

"I wanted to," Rachel choked the words out in between tears. "I really, I did... I mean I want to. I do... I... will..."

She wiped at the snot running from her leaky nose with the back of her hand. Against the commotion inside the ship, which seemed to have spilled out into the hall, Rachel also noticed flashes of light outside the window.

"This is how we will survive," the lad said as he leaned into the girl in front of him. "Look. Out there," he gestured as silent explosions erupted on multiple ships. "This will be our legacy. We will never be forgotten. We will live on not with lies but with truth. Not with deception but with reality. Not *your* reality but *our* reality."

"I don't understand," Rachel insisted. "We didn't do anything wrong."

"Maybe not you, Rachel, but the burdens of those who committed these crimes against what is left of humanity will forever be felt by what remains of your families. And your offspring. No one is innocent."

Rachel whimpered.

"It's time to get their attention. We will haunt you all until every one of you is..."

"Who are you talking about?  I am not your enemy," Rachel softly cried.

"Maybe you don't perceive yourself to be. But it's in your entitled blood. Your people certainly took long enough to help those aboard the GOLIATHs after what happened in the nebula. Open your eyes, Rachel.  Why are so many of the GOLIATHs still back in the nebula while the fleet is light years ahead? But that's what you and your kind do.  Everything is theater.  Then you clap yourselves on the back for maintaining the façade, the lies.  You tell yourselves that what was done was right and just.  That the end justified the means.  That it was all for the greater good."

Rachel gripped the elder boy's thick wrist.  "I am not responsible for whatever crimes you think my father or members of the New Earth Transnational Republic committed.  Right or wrong, they did what they had to do."

"Wait. You're not related to Captain Ramos, are you?"

Rachel pursed her lips. "He's my father."

"So then he commands a ship?"

Her hair still balled up tightly in the boy's grasp, she held her breath and nodded as best she could. "The GALAXY III."

The young man smiled as the realization of her words, and who she was, struck him. He drew her head close to steady her amid her slaps and protestations. "Well, then," he said, forcing the steel to her temple. "Allow me to impart a message for you to deliver to your dear old dad. Tell him GOLIATH IX is coming for him. We're coming for them all."

\* \* \*

Rachel Ramos jerked awake out of breath and bathed in perspiration to the buzzing of her D.I.D. clock alarm.

It was Monday morning. In her stateroom aboard the shuttle, she had less than two hours before meeting up with the YUÀN BÓ, a schooling vessel.

Partially buried under a sheet, she focused on catching her breath before kicking it off. Still racing with images from her dream, she tried to make sense of the mental clutter that frightened her.

"Room. Morning sunrise. Begin at setting two," she called out.

The far wall across from her disintegrated into her favorite morning setting, pre-synced with her D.I.D. As if she was dockside observing the rising sun over Prime Earth's eastern waters of Cape Cod, Massachusetts, the room was bathed in a dull light that was set to brighten as the sun rose.

Rachel watched as a fishing trawler headed out to sea. She had grown up watching this scene, often with her dad. It was also his favorite since he was a child. Her grandfather was the last of her family to live on the water. Live on Earth. As a boy. A third-generation fisherman, it was her grandfather's uncle's trawler in the video.

---

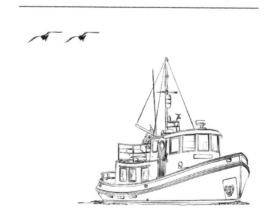

Closing her eyes, she listened to the gulls squawking in the background. The sound of the waves brushing up against the shore soothed her.

Grabbing for her eyeglasses on the end table near the bed with trembling hands, Rachel knocked over the antique greeting card she had opened the night before. It was from her father wishing her luck on her first day of teaching. It was a kind gesture, especially since he went out of his way to find such a rare handheld token instead of sending her the traditional digital version. But she still questioned how much confidence he had in her. A military man, he never shied from voicing his regret with having a daughter at every chance. Rachel, ever the tomboy, did everything she could to make up for it. But her petite frame betrayed her.

Slipping her feet into oversized slippers, she stood to make her way to the bathroom to splash cool water on her face. She was still unnerved by her dream and the emotions they dredged up so soon before her first teaching assignment.

Though her father tried to shield her from the latest news involving a ship lost in the nebula, it was nearly impossible with so many things going amiss recently. Even without the details, she knew something was wrong. Very wrong. More resources and food were scheduled to be rationed on certain vessels while technology issues were limiting necessary functions throughout the entire convoy. Excessive wear and tear on the ships, especially after the jumps, required evermore attention and maintenance. Prolonged radiation bombardment, heavier than anticipated in certain areas, didn't help.

Living conditions for some felt more like survival than living. This led to anxiety. Fear. Depression. It jeopardized the mission. Brought about discord. Dissension was spreading like wildfire through the fleet as problems persisted. With the latest incident in the nebula, the colony was fractured more than it had ever been since the generation that devised the plan to leave planet Earth and take to the stars for another home. As hope evaporated, so too did their chances of survival.

But Rachel was determined to be strong in front of her students. No matter what happened, she was prepared to be that figure students could turn to in times of crisis.

"Illuminate. Setting five," Rachel commanded as she entered the small washroom.

That's when she saw it. Reflected in the mirror. Above the corner of her left eye a large ugly gash was starting to bleed.

# TABITHA

**W**hen Jesse looked my way, I knew then that this was not going to go down as planned.

"She's not here," Jesse said, putting his hand over his eyes to shield the noon-day sun.

I nodded. Instead of using words, I just spat into the wind.

"Do you think she went with her folks?" Jesse asked.

I'm not sure he was talking to me or just verbalizing what was going through his head at the moment. He was worried about her safety. We both were.

His concern made sense. Everything had changed because of the virus. In lockdown mode, no one was supposed to go anywhere. But Jesse's girl, Tabitha, lived on a farm far away from everyone. There was no one around for miles. All Jesse knew was that Tabitha's parents were worried about her mother's elderly folks over the state border.

By this time, I had pulled my face mask back over my mouth. Instinct? Habit? Hard to tell these days. Didn't really matter much since these civilian face covers, required by law, needed replaceable carbon filters that many people had long run out of. This is the way it was. At least where we all lived.

"No text? Nothing on social media, huh?" I asked Jesse, fearing the answer I already knew was coming.

He was peering into the windows of the one-story farmhouse.

"Naw," he said. "Suppose that's what makes this so hard." Jesse looked at me. "Ya know?"

I again nodded. "Yeah, I know."

---

* * *

On our drive back into town, we witnessed the transformation that had occurred since the spores arrived. Millions of people, out of work now and with no relief in sight, maintained their social distancing. But those who dared to venture out in public were guarded. Defensive. Fearful. Many were armed.

Boarded up were the windows to restaurants and businesses, long since closed. Spray painted were the remaining vestiges of hope. *Temporarily Closed* the signs read. But temporary had all too quickly become permanent.

Though some classes continued online, schools were no longer in session. Teachers and administrators had their own families to worry about since everything else was closed. There was no money. Food was scarce as meat plants, factories, and supply chains dried up.

Online movies and television shows provided some escapism but there was no new programming aside from what people made from their own homes. That is, if they even had Internet access. Entertainment venues, stadiums that once seated thousands of spectators, now served as make-shift shelters and mobile food centers overseen by the military.

"It's not supposed to be this way." Jesse's voice was muffled from under the material covering his mouth, breaking the silence as we turned on to his street. His knuckles were white as he gripped the steering wheel.

I looked over to him as he slowed the car in front of his house. His eyes were moist as he turned away. Though he wanted to keep it from me, these were difficult times. It was easy to tear up now and again.

"I'd love to make a comment about how this all seems to be like a plot out of *The Walking Dead*, but I can't," I said. "It's all so surreal."

"Too real," Jesse whispered. He was still looking out his own window while I looked out my own.

The brown grass in front of Jesse's house was overgrown. Ignored, it gave the house an almost abandoned look. Actually, his entire neighborhood looked that way.

"Are any of your neighbors still here?" I asked. Earlier Jesse picked me up as I was walking to his place from my mostly deserted apartment complex. A few weeks had passed since I was last at his house. I was suddenly feeling uneasy.

"Some," Jesse replied, withdrawing the key from the ignition and opening the door to get out. "Many of them went to the government centers."

"Yeah, but they can't hold everyone..."

"Naw. The last time I saw Mickey he said people were headed to the state-run facilities at the border."

"Wait, you saw Mickey?"

"Yeah. Wasn't the same, man. Be grateful you didn't run into him."

"So, he..." I trailed off. I didn't have the heart to complete my thought aloud.

"He and his family. I've tried texting him. Maybe it's the signal. I don't know."

Now standing beside the car on Jesse's front lawn, I slammed the toe of my sneaker into the dirt.

"I'm sorry, Tyler," Jesse said as he moved closer to me. "I know she meant a lot to you."

Jesse was referring to Mickey's sister. She and I had dated in middle school. Though we broke up before high school, there still existed a bond. We had always remained friends, texting each other at night during the week. We had even planned on going to the senior prom together.

That is, until the world changed. Until an errant meteoroid skipped across the earth's atmosphere like a stone thrown across a lake.

"Let me get my things and then..." Jesse began.

I looked up at him. "And then what? We can't keep driving around. You barely found enough gas to get us out to Tabitha's place."

He met my smoldering glare but said nothing.

"Seriously, Jess," I said. "Our parents haven't returned. Most of our friends are gone. Doesn't that worry you? I mean, what else is there?"

Jesse gave me a moment to feel sorry for myself before slapping the back of his hand against my chest. He pulled his mask below his chin for a moment, revealing a wry grin. "I thought I was the only one who was allowed to freak out."

Having grown up with Jesse, he was like a brother to me. We knew how to push each other's buttons, but we also knew how to motivate each other. I half-laughed at his goofy expression.

Knowing he had succeeded in distracting me for the moment, his grin grew, spreading across his face before letting the mask snap back up over his nose and mouth. "That's the Tyler I know."

I snorted and awkwardly buried my hands into my pockets.

"Let me get some clothes. We can then head to your place and do the same. We'll figure something out."

"And Tabitha?" I asked.

Jesse placed a hand on my shoulder. "We'll find her. I have an idea where she might be."

But once we rounded the back of Jesse's house, there was hope. Our search ended before it even began.

Sitting on the steps leading up to the back porch was Tabitha in jeans and a hoodie.

"Hi, guys," she said, adjusting her neck gaiter.

# BATARAKALA

Jemma watched her husband with growing disgust as he hungrily devoured his food replicator sandwich in between gulps of synthetic beer.

"Yeah?" Carrick asked, growing impatient with Jemma's stare.

She didn't answer.

"Mm," he mumbled, finishing up. Rising from the table, Carrick brushed past Jemma and dropped his plate noisily into the compact sink.

He turned to her as he downed the remainder of ale in his cup. His eyes met her unapproving glare. "What? We gonna talk now or what?"

"This isn't working," Jemma replied, wringing her hands as she spoke. She made her way into one of the three rooms of the claustrophobic apartment designated as their living room.

"Well?" Carrick pressed, following closely behind and knowing full well what the problem was.

Jemma cursed under her breath. She was angry at her husband for putting her in this position. For making her feel insignificant. Unimportant. A non-entity. It was as if he was intentionally pushing her away.

"I've found someone else..." she blurted, regretting the words the moment they left her lips. The lie hung in the humid processed air. For a few beats there was nothing but the sound of the air processor whirring in the background. Then her sorry, lying eyes met his.

"Mm-hmm." Carrick nodded before backing out of the room.

"It's what you wanted to hear, isn't it," she said, calling out to him. She thought it was.

Carrick went into flight mode, choosing once again not to engage. As he had been doing for some time now, he grabbed another synthbeer and headed out the door into the night.

Carrick's reaction was unexpected. Jemma saw not relief, but hurt. Pain. Sadness.

"I've been such a fool," Jemma whispered to no one in the room.

# [ ~2~ ]

Toying with his last ten-credit chip, Carrick motioned for the attractive three-breasted waitress he'd been ordering from all night. Not many Earthers hung out here. In fact, few humans at all could be found on this godforsaken rock. Hospitable only for short periods of time, it was not a paradise. Located on the edge of the system, Earthers either came here to work or to hide. But like other fringe planets, it held its share of tall tales and strange happenings.

"Why do they still even use that term anymore? 'Earthers,' I mean," Carrick recalled asking the Regional Operations Manager two years earlier. Back when he and Jemma first arrived. When things were going well. When the company he worked for was solvent. When there was hope for a better life out among the stars. "It's gotta be generations since anyone from Earth has even been out this far. Besides, most everyone out here has been born on space stations."

"There are delegations that make the rounds every now and then," the manager replied shrugging his shoulders but refusing to look up from his inventory device.

Himself a crossbreed, he looked human even though he wasn't.

"Yeah, but isn't it offensive? The term is meant to mostly indicate human or homo sapien. Aren't there other species living on Earth these days?"

The manager looked annoyed. "I don't know. And I don't care. Never been. *WE* are *here*. *We* have a job to do. And *you* need to get familiar with the process. How about we focus on that?"

"Of course," Carrick obliged. But when he lifted his head with a follow-up, his supervisor seemed to read his mind.

He peered at Carrick with all four of his eyes as he delivered his warning. "Don't. Don't even ask about the stories. Don't listen to the locals. Don't make friends. Don't get caught up in their ridiculous superstitions. Because that's what they are. They are not legends. They are not myths. They are nothing more than delusions. Hallucinations. Tall tales. Got it!"

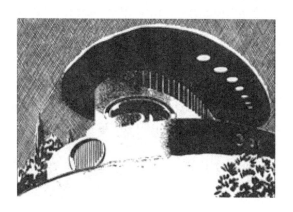

That was then.  Before the tales were proven to be more than fantastical stories told to off-worlders.  Carrick was surprised they weren't transferred sooner, that it was only after nearly fifteen months that the company finally chose to cut its losses and move on.

Stranded because the atmospheric conditions were too harsh, Carrick spent the last five months of darkness and ion storms at Crill's Casino.  Here he squandered credits gambling away his guilt and frustration while he and Jemma's relationship circled the drain.  Didn't matter the company.  He just hated being alone.

Carrick slid his right arm around the server's waist. "So, sweet stuff, when are you getting off?"

Cupping his chin, the server moved Carrick's face up from her chest to her eyes. "Think we've had enough?" was her cold response.

Carrick caught her tone and abruptly removed his arm. "Didn't seem to mind when I was piling up your tray with credits, did you now," he mumbled to himself.

Rising, he lapped up the remaining drops of his cocktail. Placing the empty cup on her tray before she had a chance to leave, he sprayed his warm, alcohol-infused breath into her face. "Ahh!"

Carrick chuckled at her displeasure. If she wasn't holding a tray, he was certain she would've slapped him.

"And I would have slapped you back," he said aloud, pausing to point at her as he headed for the door.

"Nǐ zhēn shi yīgè fèiwù," one of the patrons, a local, still at the table yelled. Whatever he had said was supported by a chorus of agreeing nods and grunts.

"What was that there, tough guy," Carrick challenged before he realized his repulsor was back in the grav and not in its holster around his waist.

"It's time for you to go home, you drunk shǎ bī," came the response as the Batarakalam stood. Some of the locals — multi-generational mixed breed transplants from other outlying planets — were large. And short tempered. This one was also well dressed.

"Right," Carrick replied before flipping his last chip onto the server's tray. "No need to get rude, Tiny."

The local growled, ready for a fight, as he came to stand beside the waitress. Her expression reminded Carrick of his wife's looks of late. A mixture of disgust and anger. Maybe even pity.

Having caused a scene, the local patrons eyed him closely until he had his helmet on and turned to exit. But not before Carrick grinned and waved at the wary group.

"Ah, hell," he blurted, tripping in his environmental suit on the way out of the casino. Unable to catch himself, he fell back into the frame of the entranceway before landing on his back.

Glancing at the digital display on his armband, he started giggling. It was only two. In the morning.

*The night*, he grinned looking at the fluorescent-colored clouds up in the sky, *was still young*.

# [ ~3~ ]

Unable to make it to the bathroom, Jemma pushed aside the mechanized mopping droid in the hall to throw up in the corner near the rear exit. Embarrassed by the mess, she began to cry. The head waitress, Katmer, an oversized crossbreed with a second set of arms, came running over.

"Oh, honey," she said, escorting Jemma to the back while wiping her up with her apron.

Turning to Charm, a young waitress who lost her family in the Ionispheric Storm of '72, Katmer whispered, "If Trahl comes, stall him."

Charm winked before continuing to the dining area with her trays of food, hearing the door to the back room close behind her.

"Alright, hon. Is it Carrick, again?" Katmer paced the cluttered office feeling all fired up. She repositioned a purplish lock behind the oversized cartilage protecting her hearing and sensory organ set within a shallow cavity while kneading her other free hands. After several messy relationships that teased an exciting life somewhere off the planet when she was younger, she could relate

Jemma was numb where she sat. She wanted to curl up in a ball and disappear. Two years since moving from Miller Orbiting Station to this outer region backwater planet and nothing was going right. None of that mattered to Jemma when the idea was first proposed because she was in love. *Still* in love, even after going against her family's wishes to marry Carrick five years earlier. Together, she believed, they'd make a life for themselves by eventually settling on one of the protective planets in the system. That is, after putting in the time here. It was a lucrative opportunity that her husband believed couldn't be passed up. Because she loved and supported him, she agreed to it.

But that was before the strange events.

Before the stories.

Before their luck changed.

Before Carrick changed.

*What a fool I was*, Jemma thought to herself. *Why am I even still even here?* She castigated herself for not leaving when she had the chance. Now it was too late. For either of them.

Katmer watched Jemma while trying to sniff a hit from one of Charm's discarded medicated cartridges she left in her locker.

Jemma used to always be the cheerful one. Lately, she was under her own private ion-charged storm cloud. Depressed, she isolated herself, engaging less and less with the girls. She had become a shell of her former self.

"Trahl is going to fire you. You know how he is with this kind of stuff at his cantina," Katmer said, fervently inhaling the drug from the tiny cartridge between her fingers. "Why don't you head outta here. We'll cover you."

Jemma wiped her nose with her left forearm. Strands of her nutmeg hair hung over her down-turned face. She toyed with a broken utensil on the dirty brown tiled floor using her foot. "It doesn't matter," she whispered while bringing her hands up to rub her belly. "I'm so sorry."

"What was that, hon," Katmer asked, her back to Jemma.

"I just don't want to see you and Charm get on Trahl's bad side because of me," Jemma uttered with a sigh. The weight she bore on her shoulders wasn't just the pressure of dealing with Trahl or Carrick. It was about what was in her belly. And what she knew about the planet. Its fate. The futility of it all. Knowing the inevitable end was near was eating her up inside.

"Trahl's here," Charm yelled from the other side of the door. "He just pulled in."

Jemma wondered if they suspected. If the locals knew. If the girls knew. It was because she didn't have the heart to bring it up to them that she kept herself isolated. Except for when she had to work.

"Mā de," Katmer uttered as she returned the cartridge with her second right hand. She used her other hands to ear dig, brush her hair, and adjust her bra strap. All at the same time. Before hugging Jemma, she quickly replaced her dirty apron with cleaner one. "Go home, hon. Go home and get some sleep. It'll provide a new perspective. I'll screen you tomorrow and we can figure this out. You're not alone in this, okay?"

Thoughts distant, Jemma managed one final glance at her co-worker.

The look initially warmed Katmer. But that feeling faded as she recognized the long-held gaze. Jemma was studying Katmer's face, taking it all in. It was one of those expressions someone gives when they are about to issue a goodbye, but they don't want to utter it aloud. "What? What is it, Jem?"

Jemma relaxed before smiling reflexively. It was an action she was used to doing a lot lately.

"Nothing. I'm good," was all she managed as she donned her exterior suit. But before securing the helmet, she paused to embrace her friend. "Wassail, Kat."

"You are acting all kinds of strange tonight. Wassail, my hon. Best hurry. Trahl will be in here before you know it."

Katmer couldn't help but feel melancholy as she watched her friend move incognito through the cantina past an unsuspecting Trahl. Beneath the toxic rain just as it was beginning its nightly cycle, Katmer watched her friend climb into a shuttle. She feared it was the last time she'd ever see Jemma.

# [ ~4~ ]

With autopilot disengaged, Carrick swerved through the intersections, a yellow blur to anyone watching the perimeter cams throughout the settlement. Taking a left onto the gridline corridor labeled Terminal View in the Main Shuttle Terminal Sector, he nearly misjudged the turn. Then when he reached the holding area, he mistook a mountain crag for a shadow. Reacting to the jolt he took to the undercarriage, Carrick jerked his Nova Class Air Cruiser, an anti-grav vehicle, to the right. Disoriented, he demolished an abandoned transit booth and uprooted a series of protected native saplings.

The young plants, too young to have yet hardened into the tall spherical trunks with thin outstretched branches that move to the planet's vibrations, were sentient beings. Locals named them Starlight Swayers because it was once thought their movements were influenced by the stars. Nevertheless, because even the locals were transplants from other worlds, the rich symbiotic relationship the trees had with its surroundings were never fully understood. Or realized. But what *was* understood was the enduring connection the swayers had to the spirit the locals believed inhabited the planet. The spirit Batarakala.

## [ ~5~ ]

"Where did you say you were headed?"

"Been offered a supervisory position for the Tsai Sheng Yeh Mining Company."

"That's great. But I hear they... Aren't they one of the few outfits that deal with outer rim territories for the Abaddon Corporation?"

"So."

"I've heard stories. That's all."

"Yeah. What else is new. We're a space station. It's a port with visitors from various systems. Everyone has a story. There are even stories about Earth Prime."

"Maybe so."

"Ever been?"

"To Earth?"

"Yeah."

"No. Seen images, though. Besides, I think Earth Prime is off limits unless you sign up for one of those special Galaxy Tours that are offered every couple of years."

"Really?"

"Yeah. The planet has become an intergalactic no fly zone or something. Anyway, Carrick, there's a lot of darkness out there."

"Makes sense."

"I don't mean just literally. Some of those fringe territories are downright unwelcoming. Many should never have been settled in the first place."

Carrick shrugged it off. "Speculation. Stories told to scare people off from stealing the planet's resources."

"I hope you're right."

"Besides the money is too good to pass up."

"Just be careful. You never know when those stories might turn out to be true."

# [ ~6~ ]

Uprooted and fully exposed to the poison falling from the sky, the swayers lay dying an agonizing death. Currently a low hum, soon their cries would be heard for miles. At full pitch, their lamentations were capable of disintegrating the eardrums of certain species within hearing distance if not safely in a vehicle or under a helmet. It wasn't just their cries above ground that were dangerous, their interconnected throbbing roots reverberated through the planet's core.

In his attempt to right the air cruiser, Carrick corrected the spin but bounced the front end off a short stone embankment with another scrape of metal to alien stone before coming to a halt.

Awake but fueled by a growing drunken rage, Carrick spun the vehicle around, kicking up loose gravel with the rear burners. His breath fogged the inside of his helmet as he scanned the area.

Alcohol wasn't the only thing that raced in his veins giving him a false sense of hyper awareness. In small quantities, breathing in the planet's toxic air offered a high that was further induced with the help of the synthahol.

Turning off his grav's lights, Carrick blocked out the shrieking plants. Instead, he focused on taking in the atmospheric radiance above the enclave. They were part of Batarakala's aurora and the neon illuminations of the planet's barred area, a byproduct of overmining.

Face flushed, Carrick closed his eyes and sat back licking his lips. Revved up, he was looking for a challenge. A release. Something that would give his life meaning. Purpose. Something everyone would remember him by. Something Jemma would remember him by.

# [ ~7~ ]

Jemma sniffled as the sad song playing within her helmet's headset ended. Her route was the farthest which meant she would be the last of the three occupants to get dropped off. But after the second passenger exited, she determined she wasn't yet ready to return home.

"Droid Driver," she said to the mechanized pilot. "Please reroute to gridline corridor Terminal View."

"Affirmative," came the immediate reply. Then "Computing. Computing. Computing."

"Is there a problem, Driver?" Jemma asked. Ever since the mining company went belly up, much of the colony's tech had fallen into disrepair. Yet the local inhabitants of the planet didn't notice. They had always managed to get by on low tech. It was only off-worlders who complained the most. They were used to more sophisticated technology.

"Terminal View is in the opposite direction of your domicile. Terminal View leads to a now abandoned way station."

"I am aware of that, Droid Driver."

They were traveling parallel to the Levitating Sea on the right, heading out to the settlement's outermost living quarters where she and Carrick lived.

"To travel outside of direct route, there will be a seventy-five percent surcharge. Please confirm course change and additional charge."

"Course change confirmed," Jemma said. With the fate that was about to befall them, Jemma didn't see that it mattered much to worry about how many credits they'd have left.

"Course correction acknowledged," the droid reported.

Jemma switched off the music with a heavy sigh as they passed a spot where she and Carrick once shared a date night. Scaling the protective barrier erected to deny access to the lethal but beautiful waterfront of the Great Levitating Sea, they had braved Allied Planetary Security.

She recalled how they talked the night away to the backdrop of floating waves that crashed against each other. Eventually she and Carrick fell asleep arm-in-arm in their suits until morning when a passing toxic rain shower woke them. It was irresponsible. Dangerous even. But romantic.

That's how it was in the early days of their arrival on Batarakala. Carrick was so excited by the move and the financial potential of their situation. And through this time, he was loving and caring. He was like a new man. Actually, he wasn't so different from the person he was when they first wed.

But that was early in their marriage. It was a time before life on the station had become tedious. Stale. Uneventful. But they couldn't afford much else. They were resigned to what they thought was their fate, their lot in life because of their lineage. Because of where they came from. It was usually only the elite — the owners, the managers, the supervisors — who lived comfortably. Even the enlisted military enjoyed a series of comforts. Not so for everyone else. That's why Carrick tried to enlist.

Coming here changed everything, including the way her husband thought of himself and viewed their life together. Motivated by the many possibilities on this new planet, every day was exhilarating.

In the beginning.

For a while.

Jemma instinctively rubbed the area of her suit that was over her belly. Together since Phase Three Schooling, she should have known that attending an engineering academy would upset him. Even early on Carrick acted like she was too good for him, though they were both raised on the same space station. And within the same vicinity.

The red flags were always there, just hiding in plain sight. Upon finishing a two-year education program, Carrick blew a chance to manage a small successful mining company on a moon only two jumps away. He claimed no one at the site liked him and, because he was the resident of an aging, outdated space station, there was a conspiracy against him. He was ultimately dismissed for repeated tardiness. Word got around that he was making his own hours and stirring up trouble with the extended-stay employees.

When Carrick returned to the station, he worked station custodial assignments before transferring to the Station Circuitry Division, assembling electronics. Dejected by lost opportunities and lofty dreams, his personality became mercurial. Easily enraged and quick with a synth drink, Carrick was fast becoming like his hot-headed dad.

Jemma, on the other hand, finished her education programs and began interviewing. That's when the cracks in their relationship truly began. She couldn't even focus on her interviews because of it, breaking down in tears at an interview for the only position she wanted.

Their time on what was officially known as J41 was going to change all that. And it did. Until the mining operation's delays and cost overruns outweighed the risks. It wasn't Carrick this time. It was the system. A system so corrupt, it chewed up her husband and spit him out.

But some of the locals said it was only a matter of time. That outlanders knew nothing about Batarakala. Because of this, they were doomed even before they began.

# [ ~8~ ]

*Awaken, Carrick Venar.*

Carrick's bloodshot eyes opened to the command uttered by a thick, throaty intonation from within his head. It was at that moment his cruiser was struck. Coming out of a drunken stupor, he became aware of an anti-grav shuttle exiting the abandoned lot. And the faint sound of the Starlight Swayers' ongoing wailings.

"You gotta be kidding me," Carrick uttered as he worked the controls to get the grav up and running. "If that *pedar sag* who just hit me thinks he can get away with it, he's got another thing coming."

* * *

Eyes wet with tears, Jemma was reminiscing about the many times her and Carrick had come here to the port in their first year. They would marvel at the ships, busy with off-world traffic, landing and taking off. How different the planet-bound landings and take-offs looked compared to the peeks they'd sneak through windows on the station.

Jemma's thoughts returned to the present when the mechanized cab operator veered abruptly to avoid the cascading stones from off the nearby rise. Though it was sudden, it was an efficient maneuver that not only avoided the rockslide but also the unsanctioned vehicle that nearly blocked the entranceway to the lot. As its programming instructed, the droid alerted Allied Planetary Security for a pickup and impound. But something else was also going on.

"Driver, what is the problem?"

"We are experiencing an internal shockwave. Obstructions imminent."

"I thought a force barrier was in place."

"The force barrier to protect any falling debris was disengaged when the lot was abandoned."

"So, we're in danger?"

"Threat reduction eighty three percent if redirected to proper route away from epicenter."

"Epicenter," Jemma asked, suddenly aware of the immediate danger. "Here? You mean the epicenter is here?"

"Affirmative. Seismic alerts issued indicate uprooted Yildiz Ağaçs."

"What?" The term was vaguely familiar. Pronounced differently by the drone, it was nearly unrecognizable from the inflected pronunciation by locals. "Wait a minute.

The Starlight Trees? You mean the sacred trees that move to the pulse of the planet? The Starlight Swayers?"

"Balance of planet disturbed. Ecosystem in state of shock. Internal reverberations increasing. They are expected to continue through a number of cycles before settling."

Jemma clutched the motion rail nearest her for support. There was no indication of the problem as they approached the area since the shuttle was one of the few fully soundproof vehicles on the planet. Even so, there had only been a few instances of imbalance in the years she and Carrick lived on the planet. But there were horror stories about what happened to the earliest settlers. And who — no, what — awakened internally to the eardrum-piercing lamentations of the Starlight Swayers.

Fearing the worst, Jemma activated her comms panel. She wasn't sure where Carrick was spending much of his time these days when he wasn't home, but she was determined to reach him.

As the shuttle exited the lot, Jemma caught more of the oncoming rockslide illuminated by the aurora lights. She was certain the grav they passed was going to be destroyed if it didn't move.

But then the grav came to life, slamming into the rear of the shuttle.

Jemma shrieked.

\* \* \*

*Now is the time to strike.*

"Yes," Carrick yelled. "I'm done taking things lying down. Enough is enough." Saliva sprayed the inside of his helmet, blurring part of his vision. He gunned the engines and made for another lunge forward.

Letting out a primal scream, Carrick's cruiser struck the shuttle's tail end a second time. Hit at an angle with just the right force, it thrust the shuttle into an uncontrolled spin.

Whirling, the shuttle impacted the metallic rock wall with a loud bang. The shuttle's lights cracked and popped as the vehicle's front end buckled into twisted metal.

\* \* \*

For reasons unknown to Jemma, the madman behind the anti-grav cruiser pivoted the craft to come around for another strike, its headlights engulfing the inside of the shuttle like a mini sun. Though the Droid Driver could adjust, Jemma was blinded until she activated her helmet's sun shield.

"Carrick!" Jemma screamed. But it was mere coincidence that she screamed his name. She couldn't see him. Not with the direct lights, the thick shadows, and the toxic rain. Jemma screamed because he was the only one in her thoughts at this darkest hour. She wished him with her. He would know what to do.

This wasn't how it all was supposed to end. She activated her message band on the arm of her suit. "Carrick, I hope I will have the chance to tell you this in person. Just in case... in case I can't, I know you tried your best. I'm sorry." She paused the recording. "Droid, why aren't we moving?"

"Vehicle disabled. Few systems... responding."

"Carrick," Jemma said, restarting the recording. "You are going to be a father. Come home. You hear me, Carrick. Come home!"

There was nothing Droid Driver could do fast enough as the cruiser's forward lights devoured the shuttle's front window. Jemma sent her message before fumbling to fasten her seat harness.

Flailing like a rag doll, her head struck the shuttle seat window as the grav collided with the passenger-vehicle head-on. Head snapping back, Jemma shattered the paned glass with her helmet.

\* \* \*

*Show your strength.*

Carrick licked his lips, the taste of metal strong on his tongue.

The alcohol in his system muted the pain. But there was no mistaking the incessant whirring sound growing louder in his head.

In the vehicle.

Outside the vehicle.

But it wasn't the Starlight Swayers.

"This is Allied Planetary Security," a voice boomed from a loudspeaker against the hard driving rain and grav engine, startling Carrick. "Power down your vehicle. Now."

Squinting, Carrick peered through the foggy, cracked helmet but found it difficult to make out much of anything. His right leg was pinned. The rancid burnt odor of toxic air reached his nostrils as he gasped, registering pain for the first time. The outside air was somehow entering his helmet. Maybe from the fall he took outside the casino. Maybe from a compromised cruiser window. Maybe both.

His own headlights now extinguished, it was the security division's periphery lights that flashed against the wet shiny metallic rock surfaces. They illuminated the inside of the grav in near-blinding bursts. He recognized it now. This wasn't the planet's aurora.

Three popping sounds from outside the driver's side door alerted Carrick to the security team's intent. He dove to the right grabbing his repulsor sidearm just as the driver's door was forcefully removed.

Something grabbed at Carrick. The interior of the Nova lit up as Carrick got off a couple of shots. But it was no use. The security detail was using a droid unit.

Held fast in the droid unit's grip, Carrick felt the sharp stab of pain that accompanies Bio Retinal Encoding scans. Though there were less invasive ways to conduct BRE scans, droids relied on efficiency, not comfort, when it came to rapidly reading identification and biomedical data.

"Carrick Venar. Supervisor. Formerly employed by the Tsai Sheng Yeh Mining Company. Power down your weapon and stand down," the droid directed.

The security team's lights revealed a team in a semi-circle aimed and ready to engage.

"You got it all wrong. They went belly-up," Carrick replied sarcastically, one leg out of his grav. The other remained stuck inside. Still tightly clutched in his right hand was his sidearm.

That's when he registered the stillness, the lack of any sound. The toxic rain wasn't falling around the immediate perimeter anymore. The security team had set up an EZS — an Environmental Zone Shell.

Used by security and medical teams, an EZS allowed them to deal with threats or traumas under, and within, a protected atmospheric canopy when in toxic environs. Even the mining team used them.

Another EZS, he noted, appeared to be in place around the twisted metal that was once a shuttle craft. Chances are the APS medical team had also seen to the swayers.

Carrick used his left hand to remove his helmet.

"Venar, Carrick, please return your helmet to its proper place."

"We're all going to die anyway. Everyone who could afford it has already left this damn rock."

An officer approached with a repulsor rifle held against his chest in his right hand, a helmet in his left. "Here. Put this on."

Also dressed in an environmental suit, his was further reinforced with material to protect against tears and even some repulsor rays. He appealed to Carrick's humanity, hoping to disarm him and remove the current threat of the night. "There's one more. There's one more ship."

Carrick obliged before shrugging, even though the gesture couldn't be seen in his oversized suit. "So they say."

"No, their arrival has been held up because of radiation surges and gravity fluctuations. At first, the directive was a precaution. This is why only company people were originally evacuated."

Carrick thought of Jemma. If he got out of this, he would come clean about his feelings. About his regret for these past months. About the love he still had for her. About how he never wanted to be alone. It was easier to push away than to be rejected.

He knew he could have been a better husband had he not felt like a failure.

Had their dreams not been shattered.

Had the world not come to an end.

Had the voice not gotten into his head.

A message from Jemma popped up on his suit's armband.

"How about we call it a night, Mr. Venar," the security officer encouraged.

As Carrick read the words, the consequence of the night's events began to crystallize. Trying to see beyond the security droid, he thrust his chin in the direction of the shuttle craft — or what was left of the vehicle.

His world. His life, as he knew it, was over.

Gutted by grief deeper than he ever thought possible, he opened his mouth to scream. The horror of the crash and the realization that he would never meet his unborn child left him without words. Without sound.

He gulped for air as hot tears spilled from widened eyes. Drawing his repulsor, he was prepared to take everyone down with him that night. Horrified by his actions, he welcomed death as penance. Anything to end the pain. The guilt.

The security droid, however, was just too fast for Carrick. Without warning or hesitation, the droid unit severed Carrick's hand at the wrist, cauterizing it at the same time. Before Carrick could even register the pain the droid also injected him with an anesthetic.

Having eliminated the threat by disarming the sobbing Carrick, the droid used one of its arms to separate the part of the vehicle pinning Carrick's right leg. It then easily plucked the driver from his precarious position.

"Carrick Venar," the security officer from earlier stepped closer to the emotionally crushed man held securely in the droid's clutches. "By order of the Eirenic Interplanetary Accords, you are hereby placed under arrest for murder. As the perpetrator in question, among the crimes that will be logged, you will be charged for the murder of off-world female, Jemma Venar. You will also be charged for the death of sentient beings indigenous to

Batarakala, known as planet designate J41.
Due to the nature of these crimes and the
presence of irrefutable evidence, there will
be no formal review. Furthermore, the
customary tribunal before your peers has
been forfeited."

# [ ~9~ ]

As Allied Planetary Security worked in
tandem with the Earth Exoplanetary
Peacekeeping Force to evacuate the
remaining settlement of outer rim planet
J41, one individual watched from a now
abandoned garrison. On the planet's surface.

"You can't do this. It's criminal."

"But you *are* a criminal."

"It's inhumane. Aren't I afforded a case
before my peers?"

"This is not a space station, Mr. Venar.
Here, on Batarakala, the APS is both judge
and jury. And you, sir, were found guilty."

The soldier looked down for a moment,
then to the main transport ship in the sky. It
was an incoming message through his
headpiece.

"Yes, sir," the soldier replied to someone
Carrick couldn't hear. Then the soldier
turned to Carrick. "A shuttle will be by

momentarily. Once our ship has departed from the port, your restraints will be disarmed."

"You can't leave me here. I'm short a hand. I can barely walk. You might as well execute me before you go, then."

"I'm sorry, Mr. Venar." Intentionally averting Carrick's eyes, the soldier opened his mouth to say something more before turning away.

"What? What is it?" Carrick asked. When the young soldier didn't answer, Carrick took a guess. "It's about the gamma ray burst, isn't it?"

The soldier avoided direct eye contact. Young, it was evident that time had not yet hardened him. Carrick could tell he was visibly shaken by what he was commanded to carry out.

"I don't have much time, do I?"

No sooner had he uttered the words did a high-altitude shuttle come into view and noisily descend on their location.

"May the gods be with you, sir," was all the soldier would utter before charging to board the hovering ship. Then it was gone.

It didn't take long for the craft to return to the main transport ship. Carrick watched the lights of the Zoyendera illuminate the derelict port as it slowly ascended.

Carrick, in high-tech traction because of his leg injury, watched everything from the window of a bunker that used to house the medical team.

Outside the rains were late. But there was a rumbling underfoot. Carrick recalled the plants screaming only a few nights earlier.

"When Jemma died," he said aloud.

*No, when you killed Jemma.* It was that gravelly voice again. *When you killed the Yildiz Ağaçs.*

Carrick seemed to understand now. He wasn't going mad. It was said these outer rim planets were possessed with beings. Some malevolent. Interesting considering whatever was communicating directly with him in his head didn't seem to show up until after he had struck the Starlight Swayers.

*I was awakened*, the voice clarified. *You awakened me when you murdered my children.*

Stepping outside Carrick noted how quiet it was. Too quiet, as a once distant glow began to illuminate the darkened skies.

"The gamma rays," Carrick guessed aloud.

*A reckoning*, the voice corrected.

Smiling, Carrick used his one working hand to remove his helmet while reciting a passage he recalled from the *Book of Batarakala*. "The trail they undertake will be murky and treacherous. They will falter and fail. For I will bring calamity upon them. A day of reckoning is coming. The Lord Batarakala affirms it!"

Zigzagging cracks cut across the doomed planet as the surface buckled, sending its indigenous life scurrying. With pockets of gravity disrupted, the Great Levitating Sea separated. Large thick waves thinned, dispersing into sky and space leaving strange uncatalogued sea creatures Carrick never knew existed to drift aimlessly about as they writhed in agony, gasping for air.

Knowing their end was near, the world's remaining sentient plants violently swayed from their stationary positions. Protesting what was coming, they loudly mourned in unison. Strange sounds carried over — and through — the planet. Tormented by their painful melody, the voice that spoke to Carrick, the voice Carrick had awakened, joined them.

---

Blood streamed from Carrick's ears as the shrieking wails burst his eardrums. Lifting his arms up to the sky, he joined the chorus as they all embraced the end.

The supernova's gamma ray burst — on a journey from a collapsed star in a neighboring system — punched right through the planet's core, sending violent shockwaves rippling throughout the planet.

From aboard the Zoyendera, just as the craft's Faster-Than-Light drive powered up, the passengers witnessed the outer rim planet, Batarakala, explode into a magnificent ball of light and rock.

# ROGUE MOON

The captain stroked his chin, feeling the coarse hairs of his goatee beneath his fingertips.

"Back off. Back off," he directed. This was neither the place nor the time for over confidence.

His helmsman, a recruit fresh from the space academy, slowed the massive starship, Apricus. Everyone felt the ship rock as it came to an abrupt halt. That unmistakable rocking feeling was a sensation that all space explorers carried with them when they returned to terra firma, especially at night when they closed their eyes to sleep.

Captain Zarek was very much aware that all eyes were on him. Not only was he and his crew breaking in a state-of-the-art space vessel, but they were doing so with an untested leader.

"Well, that's not entirely true," his wife said to him before he left for the year-long mission.

"Not like this, though," he countered. "And it is rare for someone like myself to have the opportunity to rise so easily through the ranks."

"I don't know, Zarek. You've never let your stature hold you back. After all, it was your quick thinking — your intelligence — that saved the planet when Earth's defenses failed. Instead of mankind dealing with the aftermath of a planet killer, it was you who found a way to break up the mammoth asteroid *before* it decimated the planet and us with it."

"I was young," Zarek said as he smiled at his wife, Mina, cupping her face in his hands. "An idealist." He cherished this woman before him. His companion of twenty years. The mother of his three children. His most ardent supporter. "It also helped to be in the right place at the right time."

Prior to the event, US Space Force generals had been unsuccessful in their attempts to dissuade powerful leaders from the United States — and abroad — with close financial ties to large corporations from using the situation for financial gain. They chose greed over safety, monetizing the catastrophe to benefit themselves over the lives of billions at risk.

"It would have been a crime to let such a disaster go to waste," a CEO brazenly confessed in an open hearing streamed by billions over the planet. "And had we amassed what we had intended, we could have remade the world. We would have been seen as visionaries, not villains."

In some ways the CEO was not incorrect. The world *was* remade. To Zarek's surprise, the aftermath resulted in sweeping global change. It was *the* greatest upheaval since World War II, reshaping every continent, every country. Instead of war and conflict as the catalyst or the result, citizens of nearly every nation rose to be heard. Less popular was the '*us vs them*' mentality.

It was a profound shift from what existed before brought on by a united civilization. The consolidation of separate countries under a world government leadership system stimulated a truly global economy. Universal health care, universal income, and a universal educational system were also established. It was a sweeping paradigm that brought about immediate changes in attitudes, purpose, and quality of life. Whereas in the past such a new world order would have left many feeling it a suspicious attempt to control the masses or centralize the world's resources and wealth for purposes of corruptible power, the near-death experience of an entire population exposed the fragility of mankind's existence, aligning them in the process as never before. In the aftermath, an unprecedented spirit of universal cooperation in the form of democratized socialism was welcomed.

Wanting a better life, citizens were willing to hold their leaders and their countrymen accountable.

There was no going back. Only *together* would their home planet heal, rebuild, and thrive. Only *united* would the human race be ready for the next cataclysmic event.

And though there were few outliers, the minority in this newly formed global society either conformed or faced exile.

---

Following the 'The Event,' Zarek was given the opportunity to write his own ticket. Like George Washington at the dawn of a newly formed United States of America, his legacy could have been cemented as Earth's first global leader. Instead, he opted to take on an advisory role, advocating for a united Earth council to usher in this new age over a singular individual who could be much more easily corrupted. He also oversaw the implementation of an enhanced space defense program that was in its infancy. The goal: design and build a defensive exploratory fleet of sophisticated spacefaring vessels. Designs which had yet to be fully realized. Zarek's vision was of a craft that would explore, defend, and ultimately protect their home planet.

That was nearly twenty years ago. The world was on a mission. Sciences and technology realized exponential advances, even greater than Zarek foresaw, because they were working together — not against — each other towards a common goal.

* * *

"What is it," Bertram, the XO, asked upon witnessing the narrowing of Zarek's eyes.

"Sciences?" Zarek called out, his face glued to the screen before him.

"Scanning, Captain," Commander Siddharth, Science Officer, replied.

Zarek rested his elbow on the arm of his chair, cupping his chin.

"Anything, Commander Siddharth?" he asked. If the glow emitting from the rogue object was the result of a radiation surge or a power source of any kind, they needed to know.

"Inconclusive," came Siddharth's reply.

"Damn peculiar," Zarek mumbled under his breath. Speaking louder, he asked, "Are the readings inconclusive because of our instrumentation or because of what we are encountering?"

With an expression of anguish, Siddharth delivered his line utterly embarrassed. "I'm not sure, sir. I'd say it's a bit of both."

"Life signs, then?"

"Also inconclusive. Possibly present but primitive. Maybe basic building blocks. Readings keep fluctuating. As if we're being scanned at the same time. We'd need to investigate further."

"Recommendations?"

"Send in a probe, sir."

Zarek looked to his XO. There was no mistaking Bertram wanted to share something but was holding back. "Now's the time," Zarek encouraged.

Bertram straightened himself in his hover chair, an anti-grav seater used for mobility. Because of his rare genetic condition, the chair also stabilized Bertram's bones via a force-field emanating from the seater. "Can we be certain the sphere itself isn't a life form or life force?"

Zarek furrowed his brow as he registered his peer's words.

"Probes could be viewed as a threat. Possibly even an attack," Bertram warned.

"Commander Siddharth, make a note of the instrumentation in your logs. As a test vehicle, our observations will help the engineers and designers back home meet our needs and the future needs of the growing fleet."

"Aye, Captain."

"Now, about that glow?" the captain asked after requesting magnification, his focus returning to the viewscreen.

"Perhaps a remnant from the celestial body's formation. Its core is extremely active."

"So, we have a rogue moon that is still forming? Newly formed? Can you determine which?"

Siddharth shook his head. "I am unable to determine accurate readings. Without sending a probe at this time, we're getting readings that date back billions of years but there are... there are more recent readings. This thing is made of multiple layers, as if it has been continuously forming."

"Noted. Atmosphere?"

"Affirmative."

"Commander," Zarek said as he shared a knowing glance with Bertram, "possibilities of life?"

"Probable. We'd, of course, need to investigate further."

"Considerations?"

"Extreme caution, Captain," Bertram interjected. "A probe landing, even one entering the atmosphere, could introduce foreign bacteria and organic life forms into a possibly active ecosystem of some kind."

"What about synchronous orbit for further study, then?"

"Again. I can't stress enough some of these actions could be seen as a hostile if we have not yet determined what the sphere is or if it is harboring any kind of life."

"Bertram, this... *thing* has entered our solar system. Indications are that its trajectory has already altered several times. Now, they may have been minor and subtle, enough to perhaps blame solar winds or attribute to gravitational waves. But —"

"Captain, again I don't know if we're getting interference from space or if the sphere is emitting something, but our readings are getting bounced back to us. We're not reading anything now."

"Helmsman, come about. Let's see if a change in positioning makes a difference."

"Aye, Captain."

"Is that a moon?" the XO asked upon seeing the curvature of the satellite.

"Affirmative. But..." The helmsman then looked to Zarek. "It is maintaining a static rotating orbit on the dark side of the sphere."

"Continue onward. Let's see more of this planet's orbiting moon."

"That's just it. We can't."

"What do you mean we can't?"

"It won't let us."

Zarek called to another officer. "Navigations?"

"Tracking movement. The smaller body spins at double the speed of Earth, sir. Something *is* propelling both objects forward. Helmsman Jace is correct. It will not let us... it will not allow itself to be fully visible. And sir..."

"Yes, Commander."

"Current trajectory takes it deeper into our system and once again slightly askew from what has been previously projected."

Captain Zarek pursed his lips. "I want to know what is propelling or powering this thing."

"Captain, would its trajectory not indicate a purposeful path?" the XO questioned. "Would the intent to remain hidden indicate intelligence?"

"So, maybe a hollow moon? Hollow planet? A weapon of some kind?"

"Perhaps a new life form. Evasive maneuvers of fight or flight are inherent in all living things."

"Siddharth?" The captain was hoping something — anything — was coming through.

"Difficult to determine, sir, when our instruments are now not even penetrating the atmosphere," Siddharth openly acknowledged.

"Which is why it is so vital we establish what this thing is before it gets too close to Earth." Turning to the helmsman, the captain relayed an order before standing. "Helmsman, take us above the object. Let's try another position. Monitor any changes and report them immediately." He then addressed everyone on the bridge. "Keep a watchful eye. I want to know if there are any changes in rate, temp, radiation... anything."

"Aye, Captain," came the response in unison.

"Siddharth, you have the con. XO, you are with me. Bosun, contact Kennan and have him join us in the Ready Room."

* * *

Only within the last century had the concept of rogue planets hurtling through space become an accepted one. It was proven accurate after several satellites were stationed outside Goldilocks Zones following the installation of sophisticated telescopes. In the aftermath of the asteroid event, object monitoring became an obsession for the purpose of securing humankind's only home. It also forced the nations of the world to rethink their use of satellites and orbiting objects, great and small.

"What about if you come across aliens, Dad?" Zarek's youngest asked, coming to stand over his father, face flushed just thinking of the possibilities.

"Well, Mason, we know we're not alone, right? But for whatever reason other entities have chosen to steer clear of us. Maybe *we* need to go to *them*.

"Maybe we've messed up things for so long on this planet that they want nothing to do with us. You know, because of what they've observed," Zarek's precocious middle child, Baru, chimed in.

"Either way," Zarek finished, "perhaps this mission may help establish first contact."

"You think?" Mason asked.

"I don't know, son. Anything is possible..."

"What is it, Dad?" Baru asked when she noticed her father's grim expression.

Looking up from petting the family dog, a German Shepherd mix, he uttered a truth that scared him as much as actually *finding* intelligent life beyond their planet. "Well, there's always the possibility that... that there is nothing out there."

"You don't believe that?" Mason asked. "You just said there's proof that we're not alone."

"That's just it, son. I'm not sure if it's even a question of belief. In our lifetime, in all of recorded history, actually, for there not to be undeniable proof..."

"What about all those ancient texts that tell of visitors from the heavens. Pictographs, hieroglyphs..."

"Remnants. Pieces of a puzzle no one has been able to figure out. Look, I am not saying there's *nothing* out there because there have been sightings that are... that can't be explained. But..."

"But what?"

Zarek sighed heavily. "It's just that... well, there's such a multitude of possibilities. One such possibility may even be that *we* could be an extension of *them.*"

Baru smiled. Her grinning incensed her brother.

"Wait. That doesn't make sense, Dad," Mason scoffed.

"Well, now, hear me out. It could be distance. Perhaps even age. Whatever is out there, whatever — whoever — *they* are, it's also possible they've suffered because of war or because of their civilization's advanced age. Maybe, just maybe, they are us in the future... the future of the human race."

## | 2 |

In the Ready Room, the captain sat at the small conference table with his arms crossed.

"It's been some twenty years, though."

"True, but what still keeps me up at night is *when* was that asteroid sent on its way? And by whom? Or what?"

"C'mon, Zarek. You don't believe it was intentionally launched, do you?" A decades-long friendship meant they could be open with one another. And this idea that what almost struck Earth some twenty years ago was purposefully launched was ludicrous to Bertram.

"Consider, Bert, how we've been watching the heavens for so long now. Why was it never detected? It certainly wasn't on any trajectory, elliptical or otherwise. Let's not forget how past generations viewed

Oumuamua. Only recently was it confirmed that Oumuamua way back in 2017 was not some random object passing through but a foreign probe."

"My goodness, so you *do* believe the planet killer was not a matter of chance. You think it was deliberate?"

"Quite the opposite of what you shared with Mason and Baru," Kennan snuck in.

"First of all, Kennan, don't forget I was talking with your brother. He's an optimist."

"You mean idealist, like you. Unlike Baru."

Zarek smirked. "Perhaps. And, Bert, I'm not sure what I believe. Then again, not so sure what I believe is even relevant."

"Are you alone in this belief?" Bertram inquired.

"Let me put it this way: Because of what happened and thanks to new technologies in instrumentation, a top-secret committee was commissioned about eight years ago to study recent and past data. There are some in the UEC, however, who want the study suppressed because of its implications. They want more data crunched and more time spent studying the possibilities. Some of us don't accept the premise of additional time. Case in point: this new development and why we are here."

"Why is it no one wants to admit that we're not alone?" Kennan breathed with an air of disgust. "Is it seen as that much of a threat?"

Zarek addressed the two before him with a sobering thought. "Let me clarify. Think of how irresponsible we have been, as a civilization, beaming out our coordinates all this time without a way to protect ourselves should the message reach the wrong... crowd. We haven't a clue what the neighborhood is like and yet we're waving our arms, hootin' and hollerin', drawing all sorts of attention."

Bertram shrugged his shoulders. "That's one way to look at it."

"Well, the concern, the theory, is this isn't the first time we've been through this."

Kennan was bemused. "What do you mean by 'Not the first time?'"

"Earlier civilizations had advanced technology, perhaps even more advanced than ours..."

"And you think they succeeded?" Kennan asked. "Made contact?"

Zarek nodded. "Perhaps too well."

"C'mon. Really, Dad?"

"I'm not done," Zarek said. "Another working theory is the idea that someone — or some *thing* — may have been responsible for *creating* life on Earth. And maybe, just maybe, every so many millennia, they look for ways to alter it or possibly even—"

"End it," Bertram finished.

Saying nothing more for the moment, Zarek chose instead to let the scenario sink in and merely raised his eyebrows.

After a few beats, Kennan was the one to speak up first. "You think the rogue moon is related, then?"

"On this mission, what matters is only what we can track. Verify. Possibly communicate with."

"I sense a *but* coming," Bertram uttered cautiously. "Another possibility?"

"It's the lack of any readings or communication that worries me the most," Zarek said. Leaning in, he rested his elbows on his table, "Why were our scans redirected? Our instrumentation is not that archaic. Why such wild fluctuations? Why no direct contact? I mean, by the gods, why aim these lifeless rocks at our planet anyway? Is it because they shift life cycles, like the one that hit when dinosaurs roamed? Think about it. Was the planet-killing rock twenty years ago meant to end or spur evolution? Has this happened during other times in Earth's history that we're still unaware of? If so, how many times?"

"Guess it all depends on who or what survives. That is, if anything survives... survived," Kennan remarked.

Bertram nodded.

"There it is," Zarek said. "We're thinking too narrowly. Evolutionary changes take millions... BILLIONS of years. We're but a blip."

"So, you think what, Zee?" Bertram asked. "You think these massive space rocks hitting the Earth were intentional? Purposeful? If it takes thousands, if not millions, of years to traverse whatever distances then those who sent these killers are probably already dead themselves.

Perhaps the more logical conclusion is that what we're dealing with right now is a weaponized planetoid that's been hollowed out."

"Perhaps." Zarek nodded as he studied Kennan and Bertram's expressions. "Regardless, we need to determine if they are as distant as we think or as close as we fear. The situation needs to be addressed."

"Dad, if *they* aren't here anymore, where could *they* have gone?"

Turning to Kennan, Zarek circled back to the conversation Kennan overhead his father having with his two siblings. "Perhaps whatever is — or was — out there... perhaps they transcended."

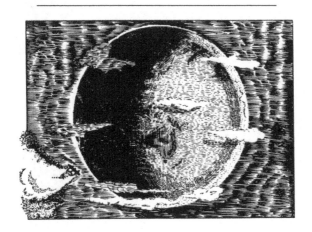

"You mean *ascended*, don't you?" Bertram corrected.

Zarek rolled his eyes as he frowned. "You know what I mean. Yeah."

"That's quite a leap," said Bertram. "Don't you think we would have found something to indicate this by now? Seems kind of..."

"New Age?" Zarek sardonically offered.

"No more new age than a wild goose chase mission in a tin cup led by a short guy as their captain, his teenage genius son as its engineer, and a scientist confined to a hoverchair as the XO."

"Wow, Kennan. How about you tell us what you really think," the XO said in response.

Kennan shrugged his shoulders. "What?"

"That was harsh, that's all," Bertram countered.

"Hey, just speaking truth," Kennan sarcastically confessed.

"I'm afraid I have to agree with my son," Zarek said, thoughtfully looking from Kennan to Bertram.

"About?"

"About this. Our time out here. Though I take umbrage with the term 'tin cup,'" Zarek said winking at Kennan, "this *is* a wild goose chase. Maybe even..." he paused as he painfully looked at his eldest. "Don't tell your mother I said this, but... this could even be a suicidal one."

The XO wasn't buying it. "We're aware of the elements of danger involved, but getting a bit melodramatic, aren't we?"

"Call it a hunch. There is even more I'd like to share but it remains classified for the moment. We should really be out here accompanied by a military convoy."

"C'mon, Zarek. After all these years of probing and building on the moon and on Mars... nothing. Nada. We have mining colonies on Saturn's moon, Mima, and a sizable research facility on Jupiter's moon, Ganymede. Again, nothing. While we've found some primitive life on other moons, they've been rudimentary. Every other promising sign indicates life possibilities from long ago and nothing of a higher order or marked intelligence. And each time we've seemed close to making some kind of contact, it's been nothing more than false alarms. Wouldn't something have made itself fully known to the human race by now?"

"Or," the captain began slowly, "our instruments cannot recognize life forms that exist beyond our understanding and comprehension. Intentionally or not, maybe it's hiding in plain sight."

"Ya think?" Kennan mused. It was a theory he strongly advocated but was ignored, even after conducting research in the field and publishing his findings. Though society had advanced, there still existed a bias against young geniuses lacking practical experience.

"I do, Kennan. That's why I've always supported your hypothesis. These are unprecedented times. We've made incredible advancements in science and technology. I mean, it took less than twenty years to build a vessel worthy of traversing the cosmos, not just transporting or shipping but actually navigating and exploring. We're not even the same society we once were before the event. But this... it's always been a subject off limits because it is such a gray area."

"A cover up," Kennan offered.

"No," Zarek clarified. "It's difficult to explain because the optics appear that way. There are some who just don't want to see mass hysteria after all the progress that's been made. And with competing theories, of which neither may be accurate, it behooves the UEC to proceed cautiously. I mean I get it. But I think it's something worth looking into. And I am telling you because I believe it connects to what we're watching out there at this very moment."

"Where to begin then, Captain?" Kennan asked.

"I leave that up to you two. Kennan, you're the youngest engineer to ever oversee a department aboard a starship. Between the two of you with your many science and engineering degrees, I am confident you can gather a team ready to address these new challenges by creating instrumentation to read things in a variety of ways outside of what is known via our existing models."

"It may be prudent to get access to that declassified material you mentioned," Bertram suggested.

"I agree but unless this thing we're monitoring becomes a major problem, we may need to keep our efforts under the radar."

"A slippery slope once we start on this path," Bertram acknowledged. "There's no telling what we may end up discovering."

"We need to use science to guide us here. The ramifications that we may not be in control, that each evolution was intentional and not accidental... yeah, could be a slippery slope. A flat earth, round earth kind of slope. But the immediate concern is instrumentation to read what may only be days from Earth. Because if it is being steered, does this mean the rogue moon is something malevolent or a weapon of some kind? Or is merely a probe? I... *we*... need to know. Is that clear?"

"Understood. I'll head back to Engineering. I already have some ideas I'd like to explore and then I will reach out to you," Kennan said as looked at the XO before exiting the room. He then headed off in the opposite direction of the bridge.

Just as the XO powered his hoverchair out of standby, the captain's earpiece buzzed.

"Go! Zarek here." Pressing the side of it to engage the device, his navigations officer suggested he and the XO return to the bridge.

"The sphere... the planet... is changing course," the navigations officer conveyed. The urgency was unmistakable in his tone. "And it's picking up speed."

"We're on our way," Zarek said as he and Bertram exited the Ready Room to make their way to the command center. "Match its speed and course. Have Siddharth run another scan."

"Captain, I have," Siddharth acknowledged before dropping a bomb on them all. "We may have another problem."

"Go ahead."

"The planet appears to be..."

"Appears to be what, Siddharth?" the captain asked.

"Powering up, sir. It appears to be powering up."

"Still think I was being melodramatic?" Zarek asked his XO as he passed him to take the lead on the way to the bridge.

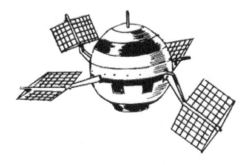

# ABOUT THE AUTHOR

A rabid fan of science fiction, Ray LeCara Jr, author of the science fiction YA Torn Timeline series, can be found consuming sci-fi movies and shows both old and new when not teaching. In this first collection of sci-fi short fiction, LeCara celebrates the genre in a classic way with pulp-era illustrations to complement the stories.

Once a New Englander, LeCara now lives in Washington state where UFO sightings are a common occurrence. According to 2022 National UFO Reporting Center data, these sightings outnumber those in any other state. This part of the Pacific Northwest also claims Bigfoot sightings dating back to the 1800s.

# OTHER BOOKS
# BY THIS AUTHOR

*Future Destiny*

*When Worlds Collide*

*The Forgotten Prophecy*

*From Where I Sit: A
Collection of Short Fiction*

*Dark Awakenings: A Collection
of Haunting Short Stories
(Coming late 2022)*

Made in United States
Orlando, FL
08 December 2022

25860515R00085